FISH WHEN KARMA CASHES YOU OUT

Charleston, SC
www.PalmettoPublishing.com

Fish When Karma Cashes You Out
Copyright © 2022 by Stephanie R Norman

All rights reserved

First Edition

Hardcover ISBN: 979-8-88590-236-6
Paperback ISBN: 979-8-88590-237-3
eBook ISBN: 979-8-88590-238-0

STEPHANIE R NORMAN AKA SAAHFANI

FISH WHEN KARMA CASHES YOU OUT

TABLE OF CONTENTS

DEDICATION

First of all I want to Thank God for never abandoning me even through all of my mishaps, and giving me the strength to write my first book. I dedicate my book to my three children Treyvon, Aunastie ,and Zaria each of you are the SUN behind my SHINE!!!! I love you more than words and I hope this book is a reminder that if we can dream it we can achieve it!!! It's official I'm an author.

Mom, you have been with me from the start, thanks for your unconditional love and support, your listening ear, your input, and most of all reminding me that all things are possible when we put God first. I love you!!!

Daddy I remember us going to get ice cream together and you always telling me life is what you make it!!! That stuck with me, it may have taken a while to sink in but now I put my best foot forward in every room I step in. I love you !! Now I definitely can't leave out my two brothers Terry and Andrel, I guess all those beat up games and long talks helped me to be the strong woman I am today. I love you both!!!

I thank my true friends for the motivation and being solid with me. I also send love to my friends and family that are no longer with us on earth, but forever in my heart, Aunt Pat, Grandma Bee, Grandpa Charles, Granddaddy Lonnie, Kalind, Antonio aka Derty,

Jasmine, Juliette, Aunt Bell, Aunt Lee and all my other guardian angels.

I also send love to my loved ones who are behind bars, Love you Von. Oh and I definitely can't leave out my cousin Karlin who continuously pushes me to grow everyday with those 6am phone calls. I can truly say my circle is solid!!!!!

I thank you all for your support and encouragement. I know I said thank you a lot but I am truly thankful for each and everyone of you!!!!

CHAPTER 1

"Sis, I am on my way. I'm about forty-five minutes away."

Dream was listening to one of her favorite playlists while she drove north on Interstate 85. Good music always made her feel good as she grooved with the music and enjoyed the beautiful scenery. A short while later, her phone rang. She saw it was Kim and answered.

"Damn, where are you at?" yelled Kim. "It's been like two hours, and your ass should have been here."

Dream sighed as she grinned to herself. "Well, since you are so ready, come on outside. I just got off on your exit. And bring a bottle opener with you."

Minutes later Dream pulled up and saw that Kim was not outside, but her front door was open. After what seemed like five minutes, Kim strolled out of her house, locked her front door, and got into the car. "Hello, Sis. Did you really think I would be waiting outside like I was catching a yellow school bus? And why is it so damn cold in here?" asked Kim.

"Girl, don't get in here starting with me. I'm very happy to see you too," said Dream sarcastically. "I hate when y'all start rushing me, but I'm here now, and Byron is waiting on us, so buckle up."

"Girl, I need to take the edge off. My nerves are bad. Grab that bottle of Patrón on the back seat, and open it up please, and pour it in my cup," said Dream as she reached into her shirt and pulled a plastic bag of Molly out of her bra and poured some on her tongue.

Kim replied, "Oh, OK, so that's why you're running behind on your time. You already turning up!"

Dream offered Kim some and let her know there was not much left. Kim grinned and said, "Hell yes, I want it. You know I'm Molly Montana."

"OK now, bitch, don't go crazy; I need you focused. We have some serious business to take care of," replied Dream.

Kim frowned and told Dream to stop acting like her mother and reminded her that she was more focused when she was piped up. "By the way where are we meeting Byron at?" asked Kim.

Dream let her know they would be picking him up at the Smiths on the south side at ole girl's crib. "Damn, we done talked his ass up. That's Byron calling," said Dream.

"Yo, Sis, I'm out here at the top, so don't pull up at ole girl's crib. I don't want her all in my business when y'all get here," said Byron.

Dream said OK and told Byron they would see him in a few minutes. Byron hated phones, so he was not going to say too much. He said what he had to say and quickly hung up.

Byron had been down on his luck ever since his wife had put him out. He had a thing for women and not just a few. One weekend he went missing with two twins. He had laughed and done some boasting about having a threesome with identical twins. Well, that fantasy weekend had cost him his marriage. Raina, Byron's soon-to-be ex-wife was furious when she found out her husband had gone missing with two white girls. When he returned she had thrown his personal belongings in trash bags that were waiting for him on the front porch. Due to Byron's lifestyle, everything they owned was in Raina's name. Byron still laughed about that weekend, but Dream knew that, deep inside, he regretted it. He knew Raina was a good woman who had really loved him. Now he was back up to his old tricks. He had a few different chicks he was dealing with from all walks of life who were available when he needed them. Byron could always find a place to lay his head.

His latest conquest was a dancer named Kiana, whom he became entangled with at one of the strip clubs he frequented. She was a pretty girl and quickly captured his attention as she wrapped her legs around the dance pole. He was captivated as she went into her spinning mode. It didn't take long for Byron and Kiana to start kicking it, and when they did, she lost her mind. She was accustomed to good sex, but Byron took her to a level she had never experienced. As long as he kept her with constant orgasms, she would do anything for him. Kiana lived a fantastic lifestyle and was risking it all for

Byron. She lived with her boyfriend, Badrick, who was a wealthy Jamaican. She had met him at this very club, where she had been dancing for a few years. Badrick had fallen fast for Kiana and had asked her to give up dancing. She had agreed to cut her hours and stop completely after she became his wife. Badrick really loved her, but it was obvious her feelings were not the same. When she got to the club, you would have never guessed that she had a man at home.

Kiana was the type of chick who gave women working in the club a bad reputation. There were all kinds of ladies in the club, and all of them were not bad; to some of them, this was just an easy hustle, but Kiana was a natural-born ho. She didn't even need the money but enjoyed her lifestyle, and now that she was involved with Byron, she was helping him out financially. When it came to Byron, Kiana had no boundaries. She had come up with a plan against Badrick to help bring an end to Byron's money issues. She was playing a dangerous game. This sounded like the perfect opportunity; he was with it and ready.

Kiana had made a key for Byron to gain entrance to Badrick's home and given him a layout of the home. Badrick was deep into the drug game and always kept no fewer than twenty bricks of cocaine and several pounds of weed at the house. Kiana had taken photos of everything and shown them to Byron. There was also almost $800,000 in the safe. She had given Byron all the codes for the safe, house alarm, and entrance gate. This bitch was playing a dirty game. Just the thought of it had

Dream's hands itching. Dream and Byron had hit a few licks in the past, but it had been years since and nothing of this magnitude. Dream joked and said after this, she would retire. This would be her last involvement with criminal activity. They had been planning this for months. She also knew Kim was the best person to work with them. She was loyal and wise to the streets. The three of them together made a great team.

They pulled up at the Smiths and could hear the music booming, always a party on the outside. All eyes followed Dream's car as she pulled onto Hudgins Drive. They couldn't see who was behind the tinted windows of the black Mercedes-Benz S550. Dream had invested lots of money into that car. She had taken it to Miami to a friend's shop to have it customized. Twenty-four-inch Savini wheels made it stand out. The car was definitely a showstopper. The interior was adorned with a special custom red Chanel-style quilted leather package with "Dream" stitched into the headrests of the seats.

Once everyone realized it was Dream, a few walked over to speak. It had been several years since Dream had been in the neighborhood. Most of her family had moved away, and her daughters' father had been murdered a few years after she had moved. He lived a very complicated life, and his murder still remained unsolved. His lifestyle was the main reason he and Dream had parted ways. They had been together for eight years, and they never stopped loving each other, but Dream finally had realized the everyday drama was too much for her and her girls. They had parted on good terms when

Dream relocated. She had experienced a lot from their relationship and had become a stronger woman as well as streetwise. She still had love for the people she had grown up with and always felt right at home when her feet touched her old stomping ground.

Byron was standing by the rail, smoking a blunt. Dream pulled her car over to the rail and parked. As they got out, Dream grabbed her purse with her all-black .380 Pocket Rocket; she was not about to get caught slipping. Too many people had lost their lives at the Smiths.

Kim jumped out of the car, as always dressed to impress. She was a real beauty with her brown pecan skin, a banging shape, and a face that caught everyone's attention. Her eyes held mystery but also told a story, and that smile just radiated so much joy. People were just drawn to Kim. She was wearing a lime-green Nike sweatsuit that drew attention to her curves. Her outfit was matched with a pair of orange and lime-green Airmax 95s. No one would have guessed that Kim had her baby nine-millimeter handgun right between her breasts. Kim's motto was "Safety first," so she never left home without her protection. These two were not to be fucked with, and if you did, they had something for you. For the most part, they were laid-back, but one wrong move, and it was from zero to one hundred.

It was time to talk business with Byron but not until they were all in the car. You could look at Byron and see that he had something big tucked away in his blue Champion hoodie. Kim and Dream walked over to Byron, and both took a hit from his blunt. Dream noticed nosy Worm making his way toward them. He had always had a thing for Dream but could not be trusted. Just like her car, Dream could stop traffic. She was petite and five feet three, with a booty so perfect it looked fake but was definitely real. Dream was a red-bone with hazel brown eyes and a dashing smile. People were drawn not only to her outer beauty but also to her kind and loving spirit. All the guys wanted Dream, but she never took their flirting seriously.

Dream and Byron had been friends for over twenty years, and she knew how he and his boys ran through as many girls as they could in the city. Some of them had even convinced the females to let them move in and sell drugs from their cribs. Eventually someone would snitch on them, and the mother and children were evicted. Smith Homes was government housing and would not tolerate their policy being abused. There was no way Dream would even entertain the thought of becoming romantically involved with any of them. These were her homeboys, and that's where she drew the line.

For some reason Worm continued to throw himself at her, believing he could break her down. He had been a known shyster back in the day. He was always trying to win Dream's affection and respect. One day he gave Dream what was supposed to be four ounces of crack to sell to help her in the business. He didn't want any of the profit; he just wanted to do something nice for her. At the time Dream was twenty-one and had a spot on the east side where she made her money, so she took it. She had one of her smokers test the shit out, and he passed out and almost died. Dream was so pissed she wanted to kill Worm and immediately hunted him down at his mom's place. He had refused to come out, and it was best for all of them because Dream had planned to shoot him as soon as he stepped out of the door.

She had not thought things through in her younger days. All she thought was it was time to put an end to his bullshit. Worm was always fucking with someone, and this would be his last time, and she would deal with the consequences. Byron had somehow convinced Dream to let it go. Dream was convinced that Worm had some loose screws. She had made up her mind to let what happened in the past go and not let it cloud her mind, but she would never like Worm or even be cordial to him. He would never have another opportunity to place her life in jeopardy. She turned her head as Worm grinned and headed toward her car.

CHAPTER 2

"Now Byron needs to hurry up; he knows I am not going to leave him, but sometimes he really test my patience," said Dream.

"I don't even know why you get yourself worked up, Dream. You know how Byron is. Y'all have been rocking with each other since we were peewees," replied Kim.

"That is the point, Kim. I was hoping he would have outgrown that by now. He is always somewhere, having a long conversation with someone and then running late to his next destination."

"Well, Dream, in Byron's defense it's not like we have an appointment to go do what we are about to do."

"Kim, why you got to be a smart-ass?"

"Sis, sometimes you stress for no reason; just chill. I know it's probably that Molly you took that has you anxious. You were worried about me, but you need to relax."

"I am fine, Kim. You know how I get driving from place to place, and I'm ready to get this business over with. I will be patient, but his ass needs to hurry up." They were now parked outside of Byron's sister's house because he wanted to pick up another gun.

The crazy thing was another one of Byron's chicks had been stalking his sister's house, waiting to catch Byron. He had been ignoring her calls for days, and she was pissed. She knew Dream's car and saw them when they pulled up and had crept around to the back door that she knew Byron would use. He had met his match with this one. She was a good woman but did not go for his disappearing acts. When Byron wanted to get away and get into mischief, he would slide to the neighborhood and go missing on Kay. Of course he was still married, even though he had been separated for quite some time. This was why he didn't take any of these women seriously. He enjoyed spending time with them, but they held no value for him. Dream always wondered if his plan was to reunite with his estranged wife. Dream's heart went out to Kay; she had so much potential but had lowered her standards and was losing her mind fooling with Byron.

"Pass me that bottle, Kim. I need to refill my cup; this is too much." Dream took another drink and lit her Newport. That helped to calm her down for a minute.

Byron came to the car, looking all silly, talking. "Man, I'm sorry, y'all. I did not know that crazy-ass Kay was stalking me. I'm about to leave her alone; she is too extra."

"I cannot even keep up with you and all your chicks. You still running around here, playing like you want to be a kid. You better stop fucking around with these women before you get hurt physically. And you better be glad Neca was not home because she would have politely put Kay in check for posting her ass at her crib," said Dream.

Neca was Byron's older sister, and she did not tolerate any foolishness. She had moved to the outskirts so that she would be far away from the neighborhood drama and enjoyed her peaceful life.

"I told her crazy ass that, and I don't think Neca would have been polite at all. You know how she is. I did get what I needed, so let's get out of here," replied Byron. He opened the door and got into the car. When he closed the door, he pulled out a huge gun and told them to look. They both focused their attention on him and the largest handgun either of them had ever seen. Byron was holding a silver-barrel Desert Eagle semiautomatic, known to many as the pistol that has the DNA of a rifle.

"That is a serious gun right there," said Kim.

Byron started telling them his plan. Kiana had already informed him that Badrick, her boyfriend, had just received a new shipment. He had to make a quick trip out of town, and everything was going to be put away in the house until he returned home on Friday. "Here is the key she gave me to get in the house. Do y'all know this dummy really thinks after I do this that me and her are moving to Texas to start a life together? I would never trust her; she is about as low as they come. She has no loyalty. After we finish, I'm going to call her to meet me, and I'm killing her ass." Byron always said no witnesses. It sounded so cold, but he had a good point. She was not trustworthy. So everyone knew their roles. Kim and Byron would go inside, and Dream would be on watch in the car. They had plenty of time to go over everything on their drive to the house.

The roads were so dark; there were no streetlights. The house was in the middle of nowhere, with no neighbors in sight. This was actually to their advantage. When they arrived they saw a magnificent light brick house with large white columns situated behind a huge circular driveway that was gated. The gate was open, so they were able to enter without using the code Kiana had given Byron. She had sent a photo of Badrick's flight ticket to Byron's phone so that he would know he was actually traveling. Byron was still armed and ready; this was not his first rodeo, but hopefully it would be his last. Dream pulled the car into an area where it would not be noticed in case someone drove by. Kim and Byron opened their doors and stepped out of the car. It was showtime. Dream prayed that they would be in and out quickly.

Kim and Byron split up once they entered the house. Kim was amazed as she walked through the house. It could have been featured in a home magazine. The floors were marble and shined like a sparkling new coin. She could smell the scent of fresh paint. Kiana had certainly placed her touch on everything—or maybe a decorator had made the home into a showpiece. A huge portrait of Badrick and Kiana hung on a wall. They both looked like royalty in the portrait. Now Kim was thinking, "That bitch ain't shit for real. Living in all this luxury with a man that apparently adores her, and she sets a plan in motion to rob him and leave him. I'm glad Byron is going to kill her when we finish this job."

Kim saw a bedroom to her left and went in. It appeared to be a guest room. She spotted a large floor-model jewelry chest in a corner. It was loaded with jewelry. She also saw a large shopping bag in a chair. It was empty, so she dumped all the jewelry into the bag. Now her adrenaline was pumping; this shit was easy.

Gunshots were fired! *What the fuck just happened? Why is Byron shooting? Something is wrong; this is not good.* Kim ran out of the bedroom with her gun leading the way, grabbing the bag full of jewels. *Fuck.* She saw Badrick on the floor, lying in a pool of blood. *What is he doing here?* she wondered. It turned out that he had never taken the trip out of town. He had found out months ago that Kiana was having an affair with Byron. Badrick had placed a monitor on her phone and was watching her very closely. When he saw that she had sent Byron a picture of his flight ticket, he decided to change his plans and stay home. He had Kiana drop him off at the airport, and once she left, he caught a ride back to the house and was waiting on Byron. He had even left the gate open so that the police would have quick access to enter once he notified them that a prowler was in his home. Now there he was, lying in a pool of blood.

Suddenly Kim heard sirens, and quickly they became louder. *This shit has just turned sour.* She saw Byron coming from the opposite direction, and they both raced to the door. Kim made it out and jumped into the car with Dream. Byron had gotten jammed up with the police. They had sneaked around to the back of the house and caught him.

"Dammit, Kim, what happened in there?" screamed Dream.

"Go! Go, girl! Get the fuck out of here!" hollered Kim. "Girl, the boyfriend never left. He was in there the whole time waiting. I was in a bedroom when I heard the gunshots and ran out and saw the boyfriend on the floor, laying in a pool of blood. I heard sirens getting louder and louder and knew we needed to get out of there. Byron was coming from another side of the house, and apparently the police had entered from the back and trapped him. I don't think they knew anyone else was with him. I'm glad they didn't see the car. Badrick must have called them as soon as we entered the house; it's no way they could have arrived so quickly. I'm just sick to my stomach. The only thing we got out of this was a bunch of jewels and trouble." Kim looked in the bag and saw lots of diamonds and Rolex watches but couldn't even focus on that at the moment.

"I need a Newport," said Dream as she picked up speed on the highway. "Do you have a light? I can't think straight. We must find out what's going on with Byron. This can't be good. We have a big mess on our hands. Let's get to the house; I've got to get out of this car." Dream was a nervous wreck as she drove with tears streaming down her cheeks.

"Thank God we made it here safely," said Kim once they reached the house. They went inside, and Dream said she had to run to the bathroom before she pissed on herself. Kim placed the Nordstrom shopping bag with the jewelry in it on the floor and sat down.

Dream couldn't sit still when she came out of the bathroom. She paced back and forth, smoking Newports one after another. She was angry, frightened, worried, and just overwhelmed with emotions. At this moment she just wanted to get fucked up. "Sis, can you call your peeps and see if he can bring some Molly? And I want the good shit."

Kim made the call. "He said he will meet us at the fish table in forty-five minutes."

Dream asked, "What the hell is the fish table? A seafood restaurant?"

CHAPTER 3

"Turn that shit up! Damn, that's my shit," said Dream as she jammed to her music. She was listening to one of her favorite songs by Rhianna, "Wild Thoughts." It sounded even better coming through the VVX Skar speaker system.

Kim told her they were approaching the fish table. "Pull over in the next parking lot that's closer to the building, and try to find a park close up."

"Damn, Kim, do we have to go in? Can't he just bring the stuff to us?"

"No, Dream, he's not here yet, and I want to play a little bit."

"Play what, Kim? You know we got to see what's going on with Byron."

"Dream, you know damn well it's going to be hours before we can find out anything. Please calm down, Sis."

"OK, whatever. Pass me that bottle so I can fill my cup up before we go in here."

"I'll give it to you, but you really need to slow down on the drinking. The bottle is almost empty, and I've barely drunk any of it. You have been drinking all day."

Dream rolled her eyes and filled her cup, ignoring what Kim had to say. "When this runs out, we have more wine."

"That's not the point, Dream. I just don't want you all drunk. You know how you get, and we've got too much going on for that. Can you come on, please? I need to get a good seat, and you're moving like you've got molasses in your ass."

"Kim, watch your mouth. I'm not in the mood, and the last time I checked, my legs moved my body, not yours. You can go on inside."

"Nah, let me stop playing, Sis. I'm ready. Let's go."

As soon as they stepped out of the car, the smell of marijuana filled the air. There was a red Camaro with black tinted windows parked close to them. There was no way you could see who was in that vehicle, but it was obvious that they had the loud pack. Dream noticed LED lights around the windows and doors as they approached the building. "How long are we going to be here?"

"Damn, Dream. Can you just relax? I have to meet my peeps to get the Molly you asked for, and I want to play a few dollars."

The door opened, and there stood a tall, masculine, handsome man who could have been a bodybuilder. When he spoke to the ladies, his voice sounded deep, like Barry White's. He was full of compliments as he ushered them in and gladly began to frisk them down for weapons. "You two ladies don't look like you belong here. Are you sure you're at the right place?"

"Stop it, Sam," said Kim. "Are the tables playing? I need a seat, so can you please hurry up? This is my sister, and she is not in the mood for your jokes, Sam."

Dream smiled and said hello. Sam finally finished searching them, and they walked into a large room. Kim made her way over to a window that looked like the booth at a movie theater, but instead it was a money booth. Kim pulled a green card out of her wallet and passed it to the woman behind the window and asked her to load four hundred dollars onto the card. Dream blurted out, "I hope you win something because it ain't no way I would be in here playing with my money."

"Look, Dream, I told you what I was coming to do. Now if you're going to have all that negative energy, take your ass to the car." Dream wanted to say something but just took a sip from her cup. One thing she knew for certain was nobody wanted to hear negative shit when they were gambling. Plus she wanted to see what this was all about. It seemed like they were in a club. "Soul Survivor," by Jeezy and Akon, was playing over the speaker system. No one was on the dance floor; instead they were all crowded around these arcade-looking tables. This place was like a grown-up arcade. Grown-ass men and women were tapping these buttons on every table. If you focused on the noise from all the tapping, it was annoying. That's why the music was so loud. Dream was amazed that she had never been in one of these places.

Kim walked over to a table in the back corner where no one was seated. She asked one of the runners if the table was working. She was told it worked, so Kim picked a seat and sat down. She pulled the green card back out of her purse and stuck it in the machine to load money on the table. Once the money showed up on the table's screen, she started tapping buttons just like everyone else was. Dream was sitting back, thinking, *This is some dumb shit*, but she didn't dare say a word. Dream and Kim had been rocking hard with each other since they were little girls, and one thing they would never do was argue among outsiders. So she sat there and continued to sip on her drink and watch.

She noticed plenty of people smoking, so she pulled out a Newport and lit it. At least she could smoke and drink in this crazy place while Kim banged on this damn machine. Dream couldn't take her mind off Byron, but she knew to keep her thoughts to herself. "Yes, baby, the bonus board!" screamed Kim. She sat up in her seat and became even more focused on the board. Now she wasn't tapping but was beating on the buttons. Two other guys hurried over to the table and stuck their green cards in and started beating on the buttons. Dream saw what looked like sea creatures crawling all over the screen, and when the players tapped and beat on the buttons, they were trying to shoot them. The man sitting directly across from Kim hit the button one time, and it sent a lightning bolt across the screen. The bolt caused an alligator that was crawling across the screen to burst open. The alligator started increasing dollar amounts. They went all the way up to $2,400. Another alligator burst, and this time it was Kim who had hit it. The dollar amount soared up to $3,500. Now Dream was interested; she was calculating in her head. Kim had just flipped her money eight times. Kim tapped the button a few more times and then loudly yelled, "Cash out!" A lady dressed as a waitress came to Kim and took her green card. She scanned it on a portable machine and counted Kim's money out to her. Kim looked at Dream and said, "See? Now that's what I came in here to do, so now we can leave, and my friend just called; he's outside." Dream was almost considering trying to play herself. She wanted in on some of this quick cash, but she didn't know how to play, so it was good Kim was ready to leave.

Dream took another sip of her drink as they walked out to the parking lot. Dream asked, "How did you learn how to play, and how did you find this place?"

"Girl, that crazy ex of mine, Brandon, would have me in every fish table in the city, all day and all night. It was terrible. We spent more time there than we did at home. It became our lifestyle, and one day I finally decided to play, and I've been playing ever since. To be honest this shit can be worse than a drug addiction. I have seen people lose it all behind them tables: family, jobs, homes, everything. That was the main problem with me and Brandon. One week he lost ten stacks in that bitch. I was so angry, and all he had to say was it was his money, and I needed to mind my own business. I knew then it was going to be hard to build with him, but that's a long story that I don't have the energy to tell. For the most part, I pick and choose my battles with the fish table. Like just now...that was great money; we were there less than an hour, and I made a nice profit. Take my advice, Sis. It's not a habit you want to start. Oh, I see John over there."

Dream didn't know where or who Kim was looking, but she did know where her car was, so she walked on toward it. Kim walked over to a white Range Rover and got in. Dream could not see the person in the Rover. She did not like the feeling she had as she headed to her vehicle, and once she got in, she pulled out her .380 and cocked it back so that it was ready if necessary. The vibe was not a good one in this parking lot. Too many cars and too many people on the outside. Tonight had already been crazy, and she wasn't up for any more bullshit. More than three hours had passed since Byron had been apprehended, and she needed to know what was going on.

She saw Kim jump out of the Range Rover and head her way. Dream unlocked the door so Kim could quickly get hop in. When she got in, she asked Dream if she had taken too long. "No, not really, Sis. You did good. I just get a crazy feeling in this parking lot. I'm ready to get back to the house and still trying to process everything that has happened. Why hasn't Byron called? It's been over three hours."

"Now, Dream, you know the police do what they want to do, so just calm down. Here, take some of this Molly. It's good, and it will keep you up. We can't go to sleep since you want to see what's going on with Byron."

"Bitch, you just want an excuse to get high," said Dream.

"Hold up; wait a minute. Now you asked me to make a call and get this shit. Now you want to go bipolar. I knew it: your ass been drinking all day, and now you want to talk bullshit. You know I don't need an excuse to get high. Here, bitch. Take the bag and calm your ass down."

Dream took the Molly, licked the back of her hand, poured some on it, and licked it off. "Ew, that is nasty. I think I feel it already." She grabbed her cup and took another sip to get the taste out of her mouth.

"Girl, you are so damn dramatic, but yes, it is strong. I tasted it while I was talking with John. I had to hurry and get away from him. He's rolling on them beans and wanted to talk my head off. He was talking some real business, but I told him this wasn't a good time, but we are going to get together on Monday for lunch and put a plan together. He is ready to invest in a fish table location. He doesn't want it around here. John is always starting up something. That's one thing I like about him: he is full of ambition. But like I told him, this parking lot is not a place to have a business meeting."

"Do you need anything else before we get back to the house?" asked Dream.

"Yes, stop at the corner store up here on the right. I need some 'gars."

Dream pulled into the parking lot and didn't see a single car. A light was on, so she pulled all the way up close to the door and saw a young girl behind the counter. Kim jumped out and was back in the car in a matter of minutes. "All right. We are good. I got the 'gars, so we can head to the house."

CHAPTER 4

"I see a strange number calling my phone; it's probably Byron. Hello?" said Dream.

The voice on the other end was female. "When did you start hanging up at the fish table?" It was Dream's godsister Sasha.

"How did you know I was there?"

"Girl, E. saw your car in the parking lot. You know he knows your car from any other and knows you don't allow anyone to drive it. Wasn't hard to figure it out. But, Sis, what were you doing there? It's not safe, and you need to stay away from that place. Somebody just got robbed there last week in broad daylight. The young boys have someone on the inside watching to see when people hit big. The informant calls them and describes the person and lets them know when they're on their way out the door. The boys outside trail them to their car and steal the money. The way you have to park, it seems like the place is set up for folks to be robbed. Stay away from that place."

"Damn, Sis, that is crazy. I told Kim I felt unsafe in that parking lot."

"Yep, it sure is. So keep your tail away from there. I can't have nothing happening to you, Sis."

"Well, that was my first time, and I won't be returning to that one, but I would like to try my luck at a safer location. What was E. doing there if it's that bad? And I didn't see him."

"You know how your brother-in-law moves. He just slid through to make a quick play and spotted your car. Oh, and one more thing. Why do I have to find out from him that you are here? That's weak. All I know is I better see your face before you hit the highway."

"Sis, I'm sorry. Don't be like that; I'll definitely stop by. I had to come here for some business, so this is not a leisure trip. It's all business. Kim wanted to stop up there, so that's how that happened."

"Tell Kim I said hello, and she better stay away from there. I saw her crazy ass last week on the east side at the salon. She had me laughing the whole time I was in there. That girl should be a comedian. I just love her. Well, I am about to lay down. I've got a double shift at the hospital tomorrow, so I need to get some serious rest."

"OK, Sis," said Dream. "I love you."

"I love you too," replied Sasha, and they both hung up.

Dream repeated to Kim what Sasha had said about the boys robbing at the fish table. "I already knew that," said Kim.

Now Dream was really pissed. "Why didn't you warn me? And why did we even go there? Sometimes I just don't get you, Kim."

Kim could feel the annoyance in Dream's voice. "Sis, chill. Listen. Ain't nobody up there fucking with me or anyone with me. Even though Brandon and I are not together anymore, these niggas are terrified of him. They all show me the utmost respect. Sometimes you gotta trust me."

"I do trust you, Sis, but I don't like hearing shit like that from someone else. You should have given me a heads-up."

"Dream, there was no point. I know exactly who Sasha was talking about, and them lil niggas ain't fucking with me."

"Well, I hope not. And for future reference, don't have me in the blind because I guarantee you I'm not going to hesitate to pull that trigger. Faith and Hope need me, and by any means necessary, I will make sure I'm here for them." Dream's Molly had kicked in, and she was all emotional and hyped at the same time.

"Let's see what's in the bag. We need to know what we are working with," said Dream. She had a friend in Cali who was a jeweler. His name was Omar, and she knew it was possible he would buy everything, not to mention he was all the way out on the West Coast, so that would be good to keep things from being traced back to them.

Kim poured everything on the kitchen table. "Damn, girl, you hit the jackpot on this." There were so many diamonds and jewels on the table; it was unbelievable. Even though they didn't get what they originally went in for, it was not looking like a complete loss. There was a total of fifteen Rolex watches, and some looked to be exclusive. "This man must have been a Rolex junkie," said Dream. "I wonder if they are all real."

"Well," said Kim, "I sure don't hear them ticking, and we all know Rollies don't tick."

"We sure will find out, though," said Dream. "I'm most definitely going to hit up my friend Omar with his fine ass. Omar will know; he only deals with exclusive jewelry, and I trust him. This just might be it, Sis."

The phone rang. "You have a prepaid call." That's all Dream heard. She was happy and nervous at the same time. It was the call she had been waiting for from Byron. What would he have to say? Byron was very smart and would guard what he said on the call.

He started by saying, "Sis, I'm in a bad situation. I've just been charged with first-degree attempted murder, and my bond is $500,000 cash. I have another charge for weapon of mass destruction, and that bond is $85,000, and then possession of firearm by felon the bond is $50,000. Oh, and get this, Sis. I have a warrant in Raleigh, North Carolina, so I also have a hold on me. Sis, I'm fucked."

"Bro, I don't care how bad it looks; don't talk like that. Giving up is not an option. You know your sis is not giving up on you, so you damn sure can't give up on yourself. We will get through this; I promise. I've got you. I have a really great attorney, and I will call him first thing in the morning."

"Thanks, Sis. I don't know when they might try to ship me to Raleigh, but I will keep you posted. I have my first appearance tomorrow, so I know it won't be before then. You still may want to call before you come down here just in case; you know these people do what they want once they have you in here."

"Byron, just stay strong for me. I know this is stressful, but you know what you always tell me: we don't fold under pressure; we stretch, and we stand tall, no matter what, so lift your head up and know I got you." Byron had always been solid with Dream, and she had given him the same in return. Their bond was unbreakable. They both said their good nights and ended the call.

As soon as Dream hung up the phone, Kim had questions. "Sis, is it that bad?" She could see the blank stare that Dream had on her face; she didn't know what to think.

"Dammit!" yelled Dream. "They are trying to fuck him. I feel so bad about this. We have to fix this. What a mess! I'm calling my attorney first thing in the morning. We are going to need lots of money. This is not going to be cheap." Dream lit a Newport as she paced the floor, shaking her head. Kim tried to pass her the bag of Molly. "I don't want that shit. I never should have got started. I need to be focused now more than ever. It seems like everything is falling apart."

Indeed, they had a table full of jewels, but no amount of money was worth Byron's freedom. Dream and Kim needed to come up with a plan and quickly. Dream wasn't concerned about Byron snitching them out, but she was worried that the police would figure out that he wasn't working alone and then start their own investigation. If that happened they could find out about her and Kim.

She did not even want to think about how ugly things could get; her girls did not need to lose their mother. Dream shook her head and started praying out loud as tears streamed down her face. She had been raised in the church and was not a stranger to God.

Dream's father was a well-known preacher in the South, and she was very familiar with God's word. Dream had just strayed off the path and gotten caught up in the world. She had been battling between good and evil for quite a while and was really at her wits' end. This moment had finally got her attention; it was her wake-up call. She put her cigarette out and fell to her knees as she cried and prayed. "Heavenly Father, I promise I will surrender my life to you. I know we were all wrong for our parts in this evil plan. We disobeyed your commandments; we trespassed against someone, stole from them, and had plans to murder. God, we have created a mess, and I'm so sorry. Byron is in a lot of trouble. An innocent man may be fighting for his life, and, God, only you know what may happen to me and Kim. Lord, I am sorry. Please forgive me; please forgive all of us." Dream continued to cry as she asked God to have mercy on all of them.

When Dream finished praying and stood up, Kim was standing behind her with tears in her eyes. They embraced as they both continued to cry. There was a new calmness in the atmosphere, and both ladies knew that God had heard Dream's prayer. Kim released Dream and picked up the bag of Molly from the table and carried it into the bathroom and flushed it down the toilet.

She also poured out the remaining liquor and wine. In the midst of everything, God had not abandoned them. They were the ones who had left him.

Kim continued to cry as she tried to talk. "We wasn't raised like this. We have always been some hustlers, but thieves and robbers…that's so wrong. Where did we go wrong? A man might die because of us and our greed. Byron already has a terrible record. Dream, how could we be so stupid?"

"We need to see Omar as soon as possible," said Dream. They both focused their attention back on the jewels on the table. There could have been jewelry worth over a million dollars laying in front of them. They sorted everything into groups by items to get a better idea of what they had. Dream asked Kim if she had an overnight bag to store the jewelry in. Kim left the room and returned with a Louis Vuitton carry-on bag. They packed everything and carried the bag to a safe in Kim's basement. This was their lottery ticket to make this situation better. "Girl, I need a shower. I'm going to get my overnight bag out of the car," said Dream as she walked toward the garage door.

CHAPTER 5

"Hello?"

"Hey, Ann. I was just calling to let you know that I might be here a few days longer. How are my girls?"

"Dream, they are fine. And why are you calling so early? You know we are still in bed." It was early, but Dream had woken up with Faith and Hope on her mind, and she wanted to let Ann know she would be staying a little longer than she had planned.

"Ann, don't start with me because you know if I didn't call, you would have been calling me, saying, 'It's check-out time; when are you coming home to your kids?'"

"Yes, you're probably right about that, but, baby, the girls are fine."

Dream may have done her thing in these streets from time to time, but one thing she never slacked on was raising her children. The twins were nine and would turn ten on May 31. Dream had fallen in love with them as she carried them for nine months. The morning she gave birth to her baby girls, they had given her a joy that she had never experienced. These precious girls had been placed in her care to nurture. She was a mom and wanted to be the best mom to her daughters. Her children had become her most prized possessions and gave her a sense of wholeness and a reason to push harder. Dream was determined not to fail her girls.

Ann said, "Well, I guess since you woke me, I'll stay up and get breakfast started." Ann loved to eat and could whip up a great meal in no time. "I know I was giving you a hard time about waking me, but thanks for letting me know you will be gone longer. Baby called to see when I was coming home. He says he has something special planned for me." Baby was Ann's longtime boyfriend. They were always on and off, but Ann loved Baby.

"That's sweet. Look at him, trying to be romantic. Tell him I will be home in a few days. Thanks again, Auntie; I really appreciate everything you do for us."

"You're welcome, baby. You know I love them. They are my babies, too, and I enjoy spending time here with them. We never have a dull moment. Oh, and who is Sean? Is that the one you told me you had to cut off?"

"Yes. We went on two dates, and that was enough for me to know I was not interested. On the second date, I went to the bathroom and then told him I was not feeling well and had to leave. The entire time I was talking to him, all I was thinking was, *This has got to come to an end*. It was horrible. I can't believe I slipped up and called him from my house phone one night. I haven't spoken to him in months, but he still calls. I just never pick up. What did he say to you?"

"Well, when I answered he seemed shocked and started stuttering and saying something about me being a stranger. It's obvious you all don't speak on a regular basis because he thought I was you. I told him it wasn't you and that you were not here. I know he has called at least five times since then. Now when I see his name on the caller ID, I just ignore the call. I've told you to be careful; it's some crazies out there."

"That is why I cut the date short, Auntie. Everything about him felt wrong, and I noticed his breath had a foul odor. His hygiene was definitely not to my standards. He had so much buildup on his teeth; I don't know if he has ever flossed. I was damn near disgusted."

"You are a mess, Dream. It's too early for you to have me laughing. I sure don't want to wake those girls up."

"OK, well, you asked, but I love you, and I'll see you all soon."

"All right, chile. Be safe and call me if you need me."

Dream hung up the phone. Now it was time to put a plan together.

The next call on her list was to her attorney, Max Banks. With a name like Max Banks, you knew he was going to charge a pretty penny. It was not quite eight o'clock, so she still had to wait before calling his office. Dream walked down the hallway toward the kitchen. When she passed Kim's room, she could see that she was still sleeping. Kim was not a morning person, and Dream did not dare wake her. She entered the kitchen and looked around for coffee. She found the coffee and sugar but didn't see any cream. She decided to go ahead and make the coffee and use milk. "Oh no," said Dream out loud as she tasted her cup of coffee. "This is disgusting." She needed her French vanilla cream. She would just have to drive to the coffee shop down the street.

Dream went to grab her keys and purse. She loved getting up and out early anyway. The morning air would help to clear her head, and a good cup of coffee would give her the lift that she needed. As she drove she reflected on what had happened and how now, regardless of what lay ahead, she could feel God's calming spirit on her. Dream had made some poor decisions in her life, but she had never stopped loving God; she had just strayed. She grew up in church and was always there during the week three or four times for Bible study, choir rehearsal, family night, or anything her parents felt she needed to be part of. Sundays were mandatory unless there was an illness in the family. Dream's father had been a pastor for over twenty years, so church was their lifestyle.

Dream selected from her playlist "Now Behold the Lamb," by Kirk Franklin. This was one of her favorite songs, and as it began to play, tears rolled down her face. She had already made a decision the night before that she was going to get right with God. She had allowed herself to be taken over by the street life. When she sinned, she sinned big. It shamed her to admit that her loyalty had turned from God to the bullshit in the streets. She had become a friend to God's enemy, going against everything her parents had instilled in her as a young person. Her moves and actions were not of good character; she felt horrible. When you know better, you do better. *The playtime is over*, she thought. *It's time to take back what I've allowed the enemy to take from me.*

The words of the song were saying, "Why you loved me so, I shall never know..." She knew God had kept her through so many storms, even when she had taken him for granted. The tears kept flowing; she was releasing tears from years of pain and sinful living. She was returning to her Creator, the One who still had unconditional love for her, the One she had abandoned. It was like she could feel his presence surrounding her as she listened to the song coming through her VVX speaker system. Her spirit was being renewed. Dream was overwhelmed at how she was feeling, as if she were being released from something that had been suffocating her. Less than twenty-four hours ago, she was planning and taking part in a robbery. Now here she was, ready to commit her life back to Christ.

It didn't matter to Dream how anyone else would feel about this decision she was making. All that was important was to please God and to become the best version of herself. As she pulled into the coffee shop drive-through, it looked like there were seven or eight cars in front of her; regardless, the coffee would be worth the wait. Her tears had dried up when she reached the window and placed her order. The cashier was so pleasant that Dream left her a five-dollar tip. This was going to be a wonderful day. She saw a call coming in from Kim.

"Where are you?"

"Girl, I drove to the coffee shop down the street to get a good cup of coffee. You didn't have any creamer."

"You and that damn coffee. Sorry I didn't think to have your favorite cream on hand."

"No problem, Sis. I'm good and on my way back to start getting ready for our busy day."

"Yeah, I know, girl. I'll see you when you get here. I'm going to go ahead and jump in the shower and get dressed. Drive safe, and I love you."

Dream replied that she loved her too. She smacked her lips as she sipped on her coffee. It was delicious! She noticed the car wash had cars back to back, and she would have joined the line if she didn't have more pressing business to handle. She hated a dirty car, and hers certainly needed a wash. This morning Byron and the mess they had created was her priority.

It was close to nine o'clock, so she dialed Max but got no answer. Dream left a voice mail letting him know she was in town and that it was urgent that she speak with him. As soon as she pulled into Kim's driveway, he was calling. "Good morning, Dream. How are you?"

"Well, Max, I'm great, but I have a situation. I'm going to need your help." Dream was smart and was not going into detail on the phone. You never knew if a phone was being tapped; that was one thing Byron had always stressed to her over the years, and it made sense. "Is it possible for me to come in this morning or sometime today?"

"Well, you're in luck. My calendar was blocked this week for a murder trial, but it's postponed. Can you believe the key witness was in a car accident, and now he is in the hospital in critical condition? Is that not crazy?

So let me see; my schedule is somewhat open. I have an eleven thirty, a three fifteen, and a four o'clock. Which of those times work best for you?"

"I will take the eleven thirty, and it is a little crazy how your schedule changed, but I'm glad you're able to see me today. Thank you, Max, and I will see you soon."

CHAPTER 6

Kim must have been feeling good this morning. As soon as Dream walked into the house, she could hear Monica's song "For You I Will" playing through her bedroom door. Kim loved music, and it was easy to read her mood and feel her energy by whatever she was listening to. Monica had been their favorite artist since they were little girls. They both knew every word to every one of her songs. Dream already knew that despite the circumstances, this was going to be a good day.

She went into her bedroom and pulled out her overnight bag. When she left home, she had just thrown a few outfits into her bag. Of course, she had no idea that she would be scheduling meetings with attorneys and appearing in court. Hopefully there would be something in her bag presentable for a courtroom setting. First impressions were very important, and she wanted to represent Byron well. She pulled a black bodysuit out and a pair of stonewashed blue jeans. She had a gold Gucci belt and knew her black-and-red Christian Louboutin pumps would give her the look she desired. Those shoes alone were enough to turn an ordinary outfit into something classy. Dream wanted to be prepared in case they were asked to stand as Byron's support.

Time was flying; it was now almost ten o'clock. She needed to take a quick shower. Now Kim was knocking on the door. "Girl, when did you creep back in here? I was just about to call and see where you were at."

"Sis, when I came back in, you were blasting that old-school Monica, so I didn't want to bother you. I know how you get when you are in your zone. I'm about to jump in the shower. I just pulled something together to wear, so it won't take me long. Oh, and I spoke to the attorney, and that will be our first stop."

"Well, I wasn't rushing you. I'm dressed, but I wanted to ask you which shoes you like with my outfit. I can't decide between flats or wedges."

"OK, I will help you make a decision after I take my shower." These two always gave each other a fashion check when in doubt; even if they were miles apart, they would FaceTime. It was that serious for them.

Dream walked out of the bedroom, smelling like Chanel. She had sprayed just enough to infiltrate the hallway with a sexy, intriguing scent. Kim was standing in the hall in front of a huge mirror with one wedge and one flat on her feet. She had a look of confusion on her face. Dream admired her olive jumpsuit that tied at the waist and hung very well on Kim's curvy figure. She looked very classy, with her hair pulled back in a sleek ponytail. Dream could see why she was confused about the shoes. The flats were full of colorful rhine-stones, and the shoe itself made a statement. They were unique and looked very comfortable. "There is something about the flats that grabs my attention," said Dream. Then she focused on the other foot that was covered in a tan Jimmy Choo wedge that went perfectly with her outfit. This was a hard one. "OK, which one is the most comfortable? Because they are both winners. The bling keeps grabbing my attention on those flats, but that camel tan on those wedges looks great with that olive jumpsuit."

Kim said they were both comfortable.

"We will be here the rest of the day trying to make a decision, so just wear the wedges. They are sexy and classy and give you a little height. You know I love heels for that extra height," replied Dream. She was only five feet two and enjoyed wearing heels. "You know I've been wearing heels since we were in high school," said Dream.

"How can I forget? Girl, you used to be walking through those halls sounding like one of them teachers; that has always been your style. So what did the attorney say when you called him?"

"Girl, we got lucky. He was scheduled to be in court for a murder trial, but the key witness was seriously injured in an automobile accident and is in the hospital. That freed his schedule, and he can see us at eleven thirty."

"That's kind of crazy that the key witness is in the hospital. What a coincidence," said Kim sarcastically. "I'm going to keep my opinion to myself on that situation. I am glad that he is available to help with Byron; we definitely need good representation for him. I know this was

Byron's plan, but we did go along with it, so we are just as guilty."

Dream agreed and said, "We allowed greed to take over, and we were all in on it, so it was our plan too. Everything about what we did was wrong, and now he is in a jam. I'm just praying that God gives us all another chance to make things right."

"Damn, Sis, you was just gangsta on go mode; now you've gone soft on me. Who is this person I'm talking to? Last night I thought you were just emotional from the Molly, but there is something different about you." Kim looked at Dream and saw she was crying.

"Sis, God spoke to me. He told me I'm playing with my girls' future when I make these dumb decisions, and this might be my last chance. Things are bad, but they could have gone even worse. My girls have no father. They would be devastated if they lost me to these streets. All these risks I've been taking are not fair to them. I been putting everything before God, and that has to end. You know Vanessa and Charles didn't raise me like this. Until last night I can't remember the last time I had even prayed. I'm done playing, Sis. I'm more serious than I've ever been to turn my life around. I'm not looking for validation from you or anyone else; this is personal. You may not understand it, but you will respect my decision."

Wow, thought Kim. She had no choice but to accept and respect her friend's decision. "Dream, you know I will always love you and support your decisions. Everything you have said is so true, and I know God is pleased with you."

"Thanks, Kim. I don't expect everyone to understand, but this is what I have to do; it's time. I really feel good about my decision and grateful for our friendship." They embraced and got ready to head out.

"I'm starving. Do we have time to stop for something to eat before we get to his office?" asked Kim.

"Yes, we should. There is a good chicken spot coming up if that's OK with you."

"That will be fine. I just need something. I'm surprised you haven't heard my stomach growling over here."

"I'm hungry myself. Usually after I drink coffee, I get an appetite, and you know I drunk a whole lot yesterday, so I need some grease to soak that liquor up." They pulled into the spot and saw that it was packed. It was a very popular black-owned restaurant that had been around since they were young girls. The grandfather had started the business, and now his granddaughter was managing it. They had a few locations and were still using the original recipes from the day that it had opened. They still served Kool-Aid and the best fruit punch in town. Of course it was not healthy with all that sugar, but it sure was good. Kim and Dream both ordered the crispy nuggets and fries with the special house sauce. Before Dream could pull out of the parking lot, they were both digging in their bags.

"I'm glad you stopped here," said Kim. "My stomach is happy now because it was going crazy. Damn, I almost spilled that sauce on my pants. Let me slow down."

"Yes, you better. And don't be making a mess in my car. You know I usually don't allow anyone to eat in here, but I thought you could eat without making a mess."

"Girl, don't try to treat me like I'm Hope and Faith. Nobody's going to mess up your car."

CHAPTER 7

As they entered the local bank, they walked to the elevator and hit the button for the twelfth floor, where the office of Attorney Max Banks was located. Max didn't play. His office was in the best place possible downtown. They rode the elevator in complete silence. Both ladies had a feeling of anxiety, realizing they were linked to a serious crime. The elevator chimed, and they stepped out. As they walked in, both of the ladies made sure their phones were on vibrate. Max's office was located directly across from the elevator. His receptionist was seated at a huge desk behind a glass window outside double doors leading into the office. She asked them if they had an appointment. Dream quickly told her she had an 11:30 a.m. appointment with Max Banks and that her name was Dream Zale.

She loved what her name represented. Dream meant "joyous music," and Zale meant "sea strength." Perhaps that was why she enjoyed music and spending so much time at the beach. Of course she knew without a doubt that her strength had come from God. Her dad had always told her as a child that their family had the strength of an ocean wave, and she had always clung to that. She had certainly endured a lot in these thirty-four years of her life. The last ten years had been especially strenuous. Her life could have been a top hit on the movie screen with all she had experienced. The receptionist told Dream she would let Max know she was there and offered both ladies water. They both thanked her and said no and took seats in the waiting area.

Dream's phone started to vibrate in her purse. It was Byron, and she knew she had to answer it. "Kim, I'm going to walk in the restroom. If Max comes let him know I'll be right back." She pressed three to accept the call and rushed down the hall. She heard Byron saying hello over and over. Dream finally said, "I'm sorry; I'm at the attorney's office, and I didn't want to talk in the waiting area."

"Oh, OK. Sis, thank you. I love you so much."

"Bro, you know you don't have to thank me. I'm going to do everything I can to help you. I hate that you are in this situation."

"I know, Sis. I damn sure don't want to be here either. What time did I tell you I had my first appearance?"

"You said it was at two."

"Oh no. I'm glad I called. It's at one o'clock, and I need you there. It's always better if the judge sees I have someone supporting me. Have you talked to Neca?" Neca was Byron's older sister. She disapproved of her brother's lifestyle but loved him unconditionally.

"No. I didn't want to reach out to her until you gave me the OK."

"I can respect that, but you're going to have to tell her, Sis, before she hears it from the streets. You know she will be pissed."

"Yeah, I thought about that, too, but I was waiting on you. I will stop by and see her after I leave the courthouse today."

"Oh, and, Sis, I need you to call Kay. I know she is probably thinking the worst thing possible. My phone is in the pocket on the back seat." He stopped and paused; he didn't want to say too much because these calls were being recorded. "All right, Sis. I know you busy, so handle your business. I love you and will see you in court."

"OK, Bro. I love you, too, and we will see you in a few. Keep that chin up."

As Dream walked back into the waiting area, Kim was still waiting patiently. Before Dream could sit down, Max walked out. Max was over six feet tall, with a dark complexion. He was very handsome and happily married. Dream knew Max from the east side. He was very well known from childhood for his basketball skills, and he continued to excel in junior and high school. He was offered full scholarships at several colleges not just based on his athletic ability but also on his academic scores. He loved sports, but because of the unfair consequences he had seen as a teenager for minorities, his goal was to become an attorney and help those who had made bad decisions.

Max understood that so many times, people were born into bad situations. He had been one of those people but decided his life would be different. He also wanted to make a positive difference in his community. It was in law school where he met and fell in love with his lovely wife. Those two were a power couple. Max's wife, Tamia, was a motivational speaker well known in the city and around the world. They were both doing so much in the community with their nonprofits, always reinvesting in the lives of others. Dream knew Tamia quite well and had even attended a few of her conferences.

"Good morning, Dream," Max said as he extended his hand to greet her. He also greeted Kim, and Dream introduced them.

Max replied that he remembered Kim from their younger days. "You dated one of my friends from high school. That's been over fifteen years ago, so you may not remember me. I used to ride with Jamal to the burger joint downtown where you worked."

Kim was shocked and speechless. She and Jamal had fallen hard for each other. He was her true love.

"OK, ladies. Follow me to my office."

They walked down a long hallway and stepped into an office with an amazing view of the entire downtown area. One wall was windows from the floor to the ceiling, giving the room so much natural light and a panoramic view for anyone in the office. Another wall consisted of built-in bookshelves filled with books and expensive-looking artifacts. The atmosphere was captivating. "So tell me, Dream. What's going on?"

"Well, my close friend, who is more like family to me, is in a bad situation. I can tell you what he's being charged with, but I don't have any details of what happened. He will need to fill you in on that."

"What is his name, and when was he arrested?"

"His name is Byron Thomas, and he was arrested last night, and his first appearance before a judge is today at one o'clock."

Max logged into his computer and pulled up the information he needed. "OK, his charges are first-degree murder, possession of firearm by felon, and weapon of mass destruction. I'll be honest. As you know these are serious charges, and I will need to talk with him. I will take his case if he is important to you; that goes a long way with me. I would normally charge $50,000 for a case like this, but I'll take it for $35,000. I can't promise you that I will be able to get this dismissed, but that could be a possibility. I don't care if he is guilty; I will work this out for him. You have my word on that."

Dream knew Max meant exactly what he said. He had plugs and connections on both sides, and that's exactly what Byron needed. "So, Max, my next question is: What do you need as a down payment to secure your service?"

"What can you afford to do?" asked Max.

She replied that she had $7,000 available that day. She didn't want to pay too much and throw any red flags for the Feds or IRS. She thought $7,000 was a safe number. "Do you accept personal checks, or do I need a cashier's check?"

"I do accept personal checks on a case-by-case basis, and since I know you and your family, a personal check is fine. Now I also see that Raleigh has a hold on your friend. Do you know what that's about?"

"No, I don't, but Byron should be able to answer any questions you might have. I know this is short notice, but will you be able to go to his first appearance today at one o'clock?"

"Yes. I had already decided to be there when I agreed to take his case. I'll just move my lunch around because he definitely needs me there."

"Thank you so much. Max, I feel so much better knowing we've got you on board."

Kim blurted out, "Now I remember you. Didn't you drive a red Honda Accord? I'm sorry, y'all. I know we're here for Byron, but I've been over here trying to figure out this whole time who Max is, and it finally hit me."

Max said, "Yes, ma'am. I drove the red Honda."

Kim smiled and said, "How could I forget? I would give y'all free burgers and fries all the time, especially after y'all left basketball practice. Wow, it is a small world. I always thought you would end up in the NBA."

"Well, you and a lot of other people, but God had a different plan for me."

"Well, it's good to see you, and from the looks of things, God's plan was better."

"So I will pay your secretary on our way out. When will you talk to Byron?" asked Dream.

"Since court is less than an hour away, I will have to speak with him after his first appearance."

"OK. And thanks again for moving so quickly. I appreciate you so much, and please tell your beautiful wife I said hello." The ladies got up, and Max walked them back down the long hallway. He told his secretary to create a file for Byron Thomas and that Dream would be making a payment with a personal check. She pulled her checkbook out and wrote the check. As she received the receipt, she gave a sigh of relief and said, "Thank God."

She did not want Byron left out in the cold. Now he had one of the best attorneys around. Dream and Kim both knew it was all about whom you knew when it came to this legal game, dealing with the system. It was all about money and connections. That was one of the reasons Max had decided years ago to become part of the legal system. He wanted to provide hope and second chances for his people. He knew that many minorities behind bars did not deserve to be there and did not have the resources for good representation. He wanted to change that. Max took all types of cases except those that had endangered or brought harm to children or sex offenders. He had no desire to help those types of criminals. Max had a younger sister who had been the victim of molestation, and he had no tolerance for that type of crime. The ladies entered the elevator with a feeling of relief. They discussed Max, and Kim was still in shock that he was the same teenager she would hook up with free meals back in the day.

CHAPTER 8

"I have five missed calls from John. Girl, I wonder what he wants," said Kim.

"Call him, and let's walk to that smoothie shop across the street. I want something fruity and refreshing; you know I love a good strawberry smoothie." Kim called John, and he quickly answered.

Before Kim had the chance to say anything, John said, "Damn, girl. I've been worried sick about you."

"Why? What are you talking about?"

"You must not have heard what happened at the table last night. Twelve people were killed, and I'm not sure how many are in the hospital."

"That's crazy! What happened" asked Kim.

"I don't know all the details, but I heard that Ox and his boys had a shoot-out with some niggas from the west side. Shit got ugly real fast. When I got the call, all I could think about was you. I'm glad you're safe. I heard that the guy working security on the door will let you in with your heat if you slide him a few bills. I'm just relieved to know you are safe. You know you're my chocolate drop, even though you won't give a real man a chance."

"Now, John, you know you play too much with too many different women."

"OK, maybe I entertain a few women, but that's what single men do. Maybe one day you will give a real one a chance and stop missing out. Don't forget about our meeting on Monday. We've definitely got to get together on this fish table grand opening."

"So you still want to go through with the plan, even after what happened last night?"

"Of course I do. There's money to be made, and we're about to get it. See, I'm not even trying to get that same crowd, and my security is going to be official. They messed up there. I might even hire a few bounty hunters. When you're dealing with that much money and people from all sides, security has to be official. We will go into more detail on Monday when we meet up. I'll call you later on if you're free, but I'm about to step in this barbershop."

"OK, John. Be safe, and thanks for checking on me."

"Girl, what was he talking about?"

"Sis, God spared us twice last night. He was telling me they had a terrible shoot-out inside the fish table last night. Twelve people were killed, and he does not know how many are still in the hospital. Come to find out that fresh security man will let you in with a gun if you pay him. That's some dangerous shit. If I would have known, I would have slipped him a few dollars so we could get ours in."

Dream rolled her eyes and said, "I get what you're saying, but that's a danger zone. Everybody could be strapped in there. That's too many fools in one building with too much ammo. Sasha said to stay away from there, and that's exactly what I'm going to do, and I suggest that you do the same. Thank you once again, God, for protecting us. I also say a special prayer of comfort for those families that lost loved ones in that shoot-out and also for those that were injured. Sis, this is so sad. I'm so glad we left when we did. I bet you last night when I was being delivered, things were transpiring. God works in mysterious ways. Even when we didn't deserve it, he covered us. I love him so much."

"I agree with you, Dream. We were saved twice in one night. I know it's time for me to make some changes in my life. For starters I'm going to be more mindful of the places I plant my feet. One bad decision can change your whole life. Oh, and John is throwing hints that he would like to date me."

"Well, do you like him like that?"

"I really have never thought about him like that. He has always had lots of women in his life. We have been friends for many years and know all of each other's secrets—and, Sis, he's fine. Did you see him last night in the parking lot?"

"No. What does he look like?"

"I think he favors Nas a little…just doesn't have the chipped tooth. I always tease him and tell him Nas is his twin. I really like the way he moves in a silence. He pretty much keeps to himself, has a heart of gold, and is superambitious, not to mention he has a protective spirit. He is a lot of fun to hang with; my friend is definitely official. My big issue with him is he deals with too many women. He has told me some stories about some freaky nights with multiple women. When he is popping those pills, he gets freaky-freaky, and I'm not the one to share my man with no other bitches. Messing around with me, I'll fuck around and whoop a bitch's ass in the middle of our supposed-to-be-fun time. I don't know why we are even talking about this. I can't see myself entertaining the thought of something romantic with John."

"Well, actually, Kim, it's not really that crazy. Sometimes good friends can become the best relationships. You know what they say: you need to be friends before you become lovers. I'm just saying, don't count him out. If he's as solid as you say, he probably already know what you won't tolerate in a relationship. Maybe he's getting all of his whoring out of his system before he settles down."

"I guess, but we need to hurry and finish these smoothies. It's almost time for court," said Kim as she changed the subject.

It was ten minutes before one o'clock, and the court benches were full. You could hear a pin drop; it was so quiet. And you could definitely feel the tension in the air. People were looking around to see who was there. It was crazy how the courthouse was one of those places where you usually ran into someone you didn't care to see. Kim had noticed Missy seated a few rows in front of them. Missy knew more gossip than the local news. Kim was thinking, *She probably doesn't even have a reason to be in court; the bitch is just plain damn nosy.* Kim nudged Dream and pointed to Missy. Dream rolled her eyes. She always called Missy "Miss Messy." She knew she would love to spread the news about Byron's business all through the city before she left the courthouse. That was another reason she had to go by and talk to Neca and call Kay so they wouldn't hear about Byron from the streets first.

A few minutes after one o'clock, the judge, an older woman, entered the courtroom, and the bailiff announced, "All rise!" in a loud voice. The court had officially started, and the district attorney worked her way through the docket as quickly as possible. Kim nudged Dream again, this time directing her attention to Max. He had eased his way into the courtroom without them noticing. Since this was a first-appearance court, the inmates were not being brought into the courtroom. They could be seen on a video camera.

When Byron's name was called, Dream and Kim walked to the front and stood with Max. The judge read Byron's charges. When she read, "Attempted first-degree murder," the district attorney informed her that they had a change because the victim had died while undergoing surgery at the hospital. Now this had just turned into a first-degree murder case.

Dream felt her stomach drop as if she might throw up. This was a complete shock. Kim just stood there with her poker face; no one could tell what she was thinking. Dream was thinking, *This is going to be a tough case, but thank God we have Max.* Byron's bond had been changed to one million dollars for the murder, the weapon of mass destruction had changed to $150,000, and the possession of a firearm by a felon was now $200,000. The judge stated that if Byron was convicted, he could face twenty-five years to life.

Dream looked at Byron on camera. He could read her lips as she said silently, "I love you." He gave her a slight smile and a head nod; she knew that was his way of responding back to her. This was definitely not what they were expecting to hear. Max was even caught off guard by the news. Byron went off the camera, and the next case came up. The three of them walked out of the courtroom into the hallway.

Max quickly told the ladies, "Yes, this is terrible that the victim is dead, but it may be helpful to Byron because now there are no witnesses to the crime. I can't speak too much on that right now, but I am heading to the jail to speak directly with Byron."

Kim and Dream both knew this was no time for negativity, so they chose their words wisely. Neither of them had much to say; that being said, they didn't say much at all. Both of the ladies thanked Max again for taking the case. Max told them to expect a call from him after his visit with Byron. He also reminded them that he was the best and told them not to worry. "This is personal to me now, and I will not let anyone down, and that's my promise."

All Dream could think about was that now she had to make her way to Neca. This was not going to be easy, but she had to do it. Neca had been like a mother to

Byron since they had lost their mother to cancer when she was eighteen years old. She had been praying for her brother so hard for so many years. He had slowed down a lot once he and Raina got married. After Raina put him out of the house, he had dived back into his lifestyle headfirst, even deeper than he was before. Neca had called Dream so many times, crying about her fear of losing her brother to the streets. So many of the men and women they had grown up with were either in prison or the graveyard. One thing about Neca was she was a praying woman, so she had never stopped praying for her brother.

Kim could feel Dream's energy through her silence; she tried to comfort her. Kim said, "I know you don't want to hear this, but it could be worse. He is still alive, we are still alive, and you had the money to get him the best lawyer in the city. We've got to count our blessings in the midst of the rain."

"Yes, Sis, you are right, but I wish I had talked him out of it. Friends have to tell each other when they are making a bad decision, but instead I went along with the plan with no hesitation."

"I know, Dream. So did I. We were all wrong, but beating ourselves up is not going to change anything. All we can do now is make better decisions and be here to support him through this case."

Even though Kim had a point, Dream could not help but think of the bigger picture. Badrick had a family, and his life mattered. All this had happened because of greed, and now everyone was paying for it, even her. Not only was she paying for it financially but also mentally; it was really messing with her conscience. Even though she didn't pull the trigger, his blood was on her hands. Kim didn't seem to really be disturbed by what had happened, and that really bothered Dream, but then again maybe she and Kim handled things differently. She had always been that way. Kim could be breaking down on the inside, but no one would ever know unless she told them. Kim was a warrior, and Dream admired that quality about her. These last twenty-four hours had been completely insane. Dream never hid her emotions; she was known to wear her heart on her sleeve. She kept thanking God over and over again for saving them and for waking her up out of that dark place.

It wasn't that Kim did not care, but she was tired of watching Dream beating herself up. Finally she told Dream, "Just stop it. Damn! What's done is done. The man ain't coming back. We're lucky to have our freedom, and now we have to help Byron get his. I know you had a change of heart, and I'm proud of you, but you knew the consequences when you came down here to do what we did. Now the shit is bad, and you getting all weak. I love you, but I'm getting tired of all this damn whining."

"Girl, you have some damn nerve," said Dream. "You're right. I did know what I was doing, but don't tell me how to feel. And definitely don't tell me what I can say and thank God for. You should be thanking him, too, 'cause right now I want to smack your ass for being so damn heartless."

"You know what?" said Kim. "The best thing to do is stop this conversation right now because I guarantee if you smack me, we gonna tear this fuckin' car up, and God will be my witness. Just try me!"

After that neither said a word, and Dream turned her radio up. It was best for them to both calm down for a minute. They were both upset and had different opinions. Fighting against each other was only going to make things worse, and they needed to stick together.

CHAPTER 9

If I still lived in this city, I would have probably bought a house in this neighborhood. They were less than minutes away from Neca's house. Neca had recently purchased her home that was right on the outskirts of the city. It was a beautiful spring day. Homeowners were washing their cars in their driveways, and children were playing and riding their bicycles down the sidewalks. Peacefulness filled the atmosphere. The last thing Dream wanted to do was come to Neca with this bad news, but she knew she had no other option. As she pulled into the driveway, she noticed Neca was on the side of the house, planting flowers. Byron's son and Neca's daughter were sitting on the front porch with huge ice cream cones. If you didn't want any ice cream, you would definitely change your mind, seeing how delicious theirs looked.

Kim looked at Dream, and they both shook their heads and told each other they were sorry. These two loved each other too much to let pettiness come between them. Neca looked up, noticed them, and started to make her way toward Dream's car.

"Girl, you keep this car clean. I wish I had that same discipline with mine. I know it's been a few months since I've washed mine. You would think I would be washing it now, and we won't even talk about the inside. I found a smashed honeybun in the back seat yesterday."

Dream and Kim laughed, but then Dream said, "Now, Sis, that's disgusting. What if someone had sat on it? That's crazy; you better start making people respect your car. My question is: Do you? Because if you don't, no one else will. The only people that get a pass in my car are the ones who ride in car seats, but soon as they pass the car seat stage, they will already know my rules."

"You know what, Dream? You're actually right; I treat my car so bad. When I got it, at first I was always in the detail shop; my car was so clean. But after I started dating James, I stopped caring about it."

"Now, Sis, something is wrong with that picture. Anytime a man makes you lose certain values, we might have a problem. A decent man want his woman to ride in and drive a clean car."

James didn't give a damn; he was all for himself. James was always extra baggage for Neca; he did not deserve her. He picked all his homeboys up and rode them in her Infinity truck, and most of the time, he brought it back on empty. Byron finally stepped in and kicked his ass when he caught him riding around the city in Neca's car with another woman. That was the end of Neca and James.

"I'm glad you let that go, Sis. You deserve so much better, but we all have to figure it out for ourselves. Let us get out of this car. I have something very important to talk to you about, and it's not about cars."

Neca's facial expression had quickly changed with a look of concern. "Were you with Byron last night when he came by here?" she asked. "I know he came by. I wasn't home, but he did not turn the light in the bathroom out, so I knew he had been here."

"Yes, and that is what I want to talk to you about."

They entered the house through her garage door. When they got inside, they came into the kitchen area, so all three of the ladies sat down at the table. "What's wrong?" asked Neca. "I've had a crazy feeling since last night; I did not sleep well. Where is Byron?"

"He is safe, Sis, but he is in some trouble. He was arrested last night. He is being held on a murder charge and two gun charges."

"Say what?" said Neca. "Oh my God, this can't be." She stood up and just began to cry. Dream and Kim both stood up and hugged her. Before they knew it, they were all crying.

As tough as Kim was, her emotions were starting to get the best of her. When she saw the hurt this was causing Neca, who had done nothing but love and pray for her brother, she felt where Dream was coming from. This was terrible; so many people had been affected by one bad decision. "Please tell me what you know," cried Neca.

"Well, we just left from the courthouse and came straight here. We did not know it was a murder charge until a few minutes ago when we were in court. This started as an attempted murder, but the man passed this morning. I have already retained one of the best attorneys in the city," said Dream.

"Who did you get? Max Banks?" asked Neca.

"Yes, I did. And what do you know about Max?"

"Just because I stay in the house doesn't mean I don't know about Max. He has a reputation for getting people out of some bad situations. I just don't know what to think right now. I was not expecting this, but I knew something felt strange. I made myself go outside earlier to do some yard work so that I wouldn't be in here overthinking. To be honest I don't even want to hear any more details of what happened. I just know now two families are hurting. The man who lost his life...I'll be praying for his family. Braylen has been calling his dad all day; I don't even want to tell him this right now. You know how crazy he is about his father, and when he said Byron was not answering the phone, I started to worry. We will get through this, y'all. I'm so glad that Byron has both of you. You know I just bought this house about six months ago, so my funds are limited. There is no way I would have been able to get him an attorney and definitely not Max.

"God, thank you for saving my brother's life. Please change his heart and renew his mind. Please be with the other family. Give them comfort, Lord. When will this stop? If it's not the police killing us, we are killing each other. It makes no sense; we all lose."

When Neca finished praying, she wiped her eyes and said, "Well, I've always been TTG, so there is no time for me to cry. Let me know what I need to do. Dream, you know I'm not letting up. Right or wrong, that's my brother, and I know he needs me."

"I love you, Neca, and I love the relationship you and Byron have. It's supersolid."

"That's the only way I know to be. I am my brother's keeper," said Neca.

"Do you have my phone number?" asked Dream.

"I'm not sure; let me grab my phone. If I don't, I'm going to get it." Neca left the kitchen and went upstairs to get her phone out of her bedroom.

While she was upstairs, Kim and Dream admired Neca's decorating skills. She really had her house looking like a show home. Kim joked, "Her car might be dirty, but this house is spotless."

"You're right about that. I'm so proud of her. She has worked so hard and come so far. After that relationship with James, it almost broke her."

Somewhere along the way, God had stepped in. When he did Neca looked in the mirror and straightened her crown. She was stronger than ever and accomplishing all her goals. Neca had always been a go-getter, and she refused to let any distraction waste any more of her precious time.

"OK, what's your phone number?" asked Neca as she walked back into the kitchen. "I need yours, too, Kim." They both gave her their numbers so that they could all stay in contact with each other. "How long will you be in town, Dream?"

"Really, I'm not sure; probably a few more days. I do need to get home to my girls, but I also have a few things I would like to handle before I go."

"Well, you know I'm here, so if you need me to do something, I will. We are in this together," said Kim.

"Me too," said Neca. "All you have to do is say the word."

"Thanks, y'all. Byron will probably be calling soon. I know Max was going to talk to him, so I'm curious to hear how that goes. I will call you later and let you know when I get any updates."

"Thanks. I'm going back outside to finish planting these flowers before the sun goes down. I've been thinking of starting a garden too."

"Well, whatever you do, I know it's going to be nice. You have this house looking amazing. I need you to come put your touch on mine," said Kim.

"You know I will. Did Byron tell you that I started my own interior decorating company?"

"No, he hasn't said a word."

"Yes, ma'am. I've been in business for four months now. God has truly blessed me beyond my expectations. I'm so busy that I had to quit my nine-to-five so that I could give this my complete focus."

"That's wonderful, Neca. I know you've always had a passion for decorating and Pinterest projects. You have a gift, and you can look forward to me as a new client."

"It will be my pleasure; just let me know when you are ready. Well, ladies, thanks again for stopping by to let me know what's going on."

CHAPTER 10

"Hey, Omar!"

The phone was silent for a minute. "Wait a minute. This voice sounds real familiar. Is this my dream girl?"

"Yes, Omar, this is Dream." He could hear her blushing through the phone. She couldn't deny she was flattered; Omar always had a way of making her smile. He was the only person who called her that, but she kind of liked it.

"How have you been? I was just thinking of you last week," he said.

"That's strange. If you were thinking of me, why didn't you call?" asked Dream.

"The reason I didn't call was because my phone fell in the ocean while I was Jet-Skiing. I know I should not have had it in my pocket on the water, but I forgot. To make things worse, I forgot my iCloud password, so I could not get any of my contacts. So I'm really glad that you called. I kind of looked at is God removing certain connections from my life, so I wasn't really tripping, but I promise you've been on my mind real heavy. This call has completely caught me off guard. You just don't know how happy I am to hear your voice."

"I've been great; we need to get together soon."

"Well, when you say 'soon,' what do you mean? You know I stay ready, so all you have to do is say the word."

"I just said it," said Dream.

Omar always loved how straight to the point she was.

"I have something important I want to go over with you. I'm almost one hundred percent sure that you are going to want in, but we will need to talk about it in person. If I pay for your flight, how soon can you get here?"

"Wow, you are serious. You've got my curiosity up now, and you know I can pay for my own flight."

"Yes, I'm very serious, and I didn't ask you to pay for the flight. This is business, so I will handle it."

"Well, what if I want to make it personal?" asked Omar.

"As for right now, the purpose of this trip is business, so I've got it."

"You know I'm all about my business, so find a flight, and I'm on my way. You never fail to amaze me, dream girl. I know without a doubt God sent you; one day you will realize it too. What are the odds my phone was destroyed, I lost all my contacts, and I've had you on my mind? Now today you call me out the blue. God is good. I guarantee when I see you this time, I'm not going to lose contact with you again. I think I'm going to write your phone number down on a piece of paper and put it in my wallet for emergencies."

"Omar, you are so silly."

"I'm not playing; I'm writing it down now." He was so serious. He took a picture of the paper he had written her name and number down on and sent it to her in a text message.

Dream was flattered once again, but she couldn't let him know. "Well, I'm going to get online when I get out of this car, and I'll find a flight. I will call you back before I book it to make sure that it works for you."

"OK, that's fine. Just let me know, and I'm going to start getting ready on this end."

"OK, stay safe, and I'll call you in a few." They ended the call.

Dream told Kim, "That was perfect. He is ready as soon as I book the flight. I know he is the perfect person because if he doesn't get everything, he will definitely have a buyer he is connected to on another level." Dream had met Omar years ago when she had started going to Cali to visit her cousin Wendy. Wendy had set the two of them up on a date, and even though they were very much attracted to each other, things had turned business instead. The distance played a major part; Dream just couldn't seem to take Omar seriously with them being so many miles apart. They did not speak on a regular basis, but they had a bond out of this world. Dream knew she could trust Omar without a doubt. Now all she had to do was make these travel arrangements.

"Girl, I'm hungry again," said Dream.

"I was just thinking the same thing. We haven't eaten since before court. Let's grab something on the way to the house. What do you want to eat?" asked Kim.

"I actually have a taste for that express hibachi place down the street."

"How did I know you were going to say that?"

"Well, Sis, it's not very often that I come here and don't get a plate from there. You're right; you just swear you know me like that."

"Ah, I do. We been rocking since pigtails and ponytails. Now look at us. It's been over twentysomething years, almost thirty."

"I'm so thankful to have you in my life, Kim. I always felt like you were really my sister."

"I am your sister, Dream, and I love you, too, Sis. Our families are family now because of our bond."

When they got to the restaurant, they both ordered hibachi rice with chicken and shrimp. Dream ordered hers with extra ginger sauce, and Kim ordered with the white sauce. "Before we pull off, please make sure they put my extra sauce in the bag. I don't want my rice to be dry; the sauce makes it so much better."

"Nope, they only put one in the bag."

"See? I'm glad I told you to look." They were still at the window, so Dream got the lady's attention. "Can I get another sauce, please?"

"Yes, but it's fifty cents."

Dream gave her four quarters and said, "As a matter of fact, make it two, please." She looked at Kim and asked her if she needed extra, but Kim said no. "All right. Do we have any more stops before we get to the house?"

"No, I'm good. Plus I'm ready to eat; this food smells so good."

Dream was ready to eat, too, but even more ready to find this flight for Omar. They pulled up at the house, and both of them went to take showers and change into something more comfortable. It didn't take them long to get showered and get back to the kitchen table; they were both hungry. Dream was eating and searching for flights at the same time.

"OK, so here is one that departs at one a.m. and arrives here at six fifteen a.m. It has a crazy layover in Chicago. Then I see another one that leaves at three p.m. and arrives here at six p.m. I like the arrival time better on the first flight, but I don't know how he will feel about that long layover."

"I personally don't like being in the airport on long layovers. Just call and see what he says so you can get it booked. The sooner he gets here, the faster we can get the ball rolling."

When Dream got Omar on the phone, to her surprise he preferred the first flight with the long layover. Omar said he didn't want to waste any time, and he was cool with hanging out in the airport. He said he could grab something to eat and do some work on his laptop while he waited. After she got off the phone with him, she booked the flight and sent him the itinerary.

"Girl, I'm so glad things are moving forward. I bet Omar is going to be completely shocked when he sees the reason for me flying him out here. I'm so glad that you were able to make it out of there with the jewelry. And thank God we got away from there. People wouldn't believe what we have been through in these last twenty-four hours. It's been a roller-coaster ride, and the ride still isn't over. I have a feeling that things are going to get better fast—and in a hurry. Just watch."

"I have that same feeling too," said Kim. "I also have the feeling that I'm ready to lay down. I know it's early, but honey, I'm tired. That food just did it for me. Not to mention we had a long night last night, and my body is reminding me I didn't get my proper rest."

Dream looked up at the microwave. The time read 8:18 p.m., but it seemed so much later. "Girl, I agree with you. I just want to lay in bed and get comfortable. You know we have another early morning because we have to be at the airport for Omar."

Kim went and grabbed her ashtray and lit the rest of her blunt. "Girl, this right here is going to help me to rest so good."

Dream was actually surprised because Kim had not smoked all day. Kim had been smoking since she was twelve years old. She had started when they were in middle school. Kim's boyfriend Jamal had been two years older, and he would pick her up at the bus stop and take her to school. Kim knew her mother would not allow this, so she sneaked around with Jamal for years, and they would smoke before he took her to school. She hid the fact that she was smoking weed from everybody, even Dream. Kim could be really sneaky when she wanted to. Kim was always an honors student, so the last thing anyone would have suspected was that she would be smoking weed.

Well, twenty years later, she was still smoking, and she didn't care who knew it. She said that it kept her calm and relaxed. Over the years Kim had been through so much; some events were great, and some were traumatic. The turning point was when Jamal, Kim's true love, had shot and killed himself right in front of her. He had just lost it one day. Kim had come home from work, and he was sitting on the bed with the gun to his head. As soon as she walked into the bedroom, he said goodbye and pulled the trigger. This had really fucked Kim up. To see her best friend, the man she had loved since middle school, on her bed with his brains all over their bedroom wall—it was a nightmare. She couldn't believe how quickly he was gone. And why did he have to do it in her face? That was an image that she had to live with forever.

She also blamed herself for not realizing that he was so depressed. Jamal had been planning this for a while, and she'd had no idea. He had set up a life insurance policy, making her the beneficiary, and he had left her $450,000. Kim did not even want the money; she just wanted Jamal back. When Jamal died Kim had lost part of herself. She was angry and sad. She loved Jamal more than words could describe and had never even thought of having to live without him.

After Jamal's death Dream had Kim come and stay with her. She knew there was no way that Kim would be able to stay in that house after what Jamal had done. Over the years Kim had learned to cope with the pain, but no matter what, it was still there. She had bought a home with some of the money Jamal had left. Till this day she still went to her therapist and probably would never stop. Dream was always Kim's listening ear, her shoulder to cry on, but most of all, a praying friend. Kim sat at the kitchen table and finished her blunt, then got up and gave Dream a hug. "Good night, Sis. I love you."

"I love you too."

They both walked out of the kitchen and toward their rooms. When Dream got into her room, she turned the TV to a movie channel. Even though she had experienced her own drama in real life, she was looking for a good drama movie. She found something that looked good. She also went ahead and set her alarm for 4:30 a.m. so she wouldn't be rushed picking Omar up from the airport. Dream didn't even make it through fifteen minutes of the movie before she was asleep. Max had called her phone three times, and she didn't hear it at all. He did leave a message saying he would just try her again in the morning.

CHAPTER 11

"Oh my God, it's five fifteen!" Dream had slept through her alarm. She jumped up quickly in a panic. She could not be late to pick up Omar. When she looked at her phone, she had seven missed calls, three of which were from Max. Two calls were from Omar, and the other two were from a strange number. Her body must have been extremely exhausted because she hadn't heard anything. She was just thankful that she woke up when she did. She still had enough time to make it without being late.

She walked down the hallway to Kim's room to wake her up. "Girl, I overslept! We have got to hurry up. It's five twenty now." The airport was about fifteen minutes away from Kim's house. "I'm gonna take a quick shower and throw something on; I can't be late."

"Do you really need me to ride with you?" asked Kim. "You know I hate rushing. I can stay here and make breakfast for all of us."

"You know, that is actually a good idea," said Dream. "Let me go ahead and get in the shower; I have no time to waste." Dream went back into her room and looked in her overnight bag before she got into the shower. She had an oversized black Balenciaga T-shirt and a black pair of leggings she had pulled out to wear. Dream took a very quick shower. Her grandfather had always said it only took three minutes to get clean. She usually loved long showers as a part of her cleansing and meditation time, but on this morning, she went by her grandfather's rule.

As she dried off, she washed her face and brushed her teeth. She quickly brushed her hair up into a ponytail and headed out the door. Kim must have been in the shower, but Dream wasn't about to check and see; she had to hurry up. The time was now 5:35 a.m. She was really pushing it. Hopefully traffic would be light, and she would be OK.

When Dream arrived at the airport, it was 5:55 a.m. She was finally there, but still she had to park and get to the terminal. She had found the pickup parking zone and went inside. She looked at the computer display, and to her surprise, Omar's flight, 4277, had been delayed for thirty minutes. Dream had never been so relieved to see a delayed flight. This gave her a few minutes to calm down since she had been rushing since she opened her eyes. Her phone rang; it was Kim.

"So did you make it in time?" she asked.

"Yes, barely. I just got here, but thank God his flight has a delay, so I can calm down a little." Dream knew that was God shifting things in her favor.

"Well, Sis, I was just checking on you. I know how you get when you are rushing. That was another reason I said I would stay and start on breakfast. Now you can relax a little since you have a few extra minutes before he arrives."

"Yes, you're right. I'm walking down to the terminal now so that I can find a seat while I wait."

She now had until 6:45 a.m. before Omar arrived. The airport was so crowded, with so many people traveling to different parts of the world. As Dream sat there, observing her surroundings, she began to think of her next vacation. She had wanted to go to Africa for years. Faith and Hope had never flown before. She wanted them to remember that as their first flight experience. She began to daydream of exploring Africa together with her daughters. She looked down at her watch. Time was flying; it was 6:40 a.m. Omar's flight had arrived; she could see his plane out of the window. The monitor flashed that flight 4277 had arrived. Passengers began to exit the plane.

Now Dream's attention was focused; she did not want to miss Omar exiting the plane. As soon as he walked through the exit, they immediately locked eyes with each other. It was like they felt each other's energy. Now Dream was really tripping. The two of them were damn near dressed alike. *What are the odds?* she thought. Omar was dressed in Balenciaga from head to toe. He wore a Balenciaga logo print hoodie with a pair of black sweatpants. He finished the look off with his Triple S sneakers. As he looked at Dream, you could tell he was thinking the same thing. They were not a couple, but if you looked at them, you definitely would have thought differently. They walked toward each other and hugged.

The first thing out of Omar's mouth was "Good morning, twin."

Dream laughed. "Well, you know they say great minds think alike."

"It's good to see we are starting our morning off on the same page."

"I really just grabbed something quick to put on. I actually missed my alarm and was running late. So to be honest, I didn't put much thought into this outfit."

"Neither did I. I just grabbed a hoodie because I know the planes are usually cold. Well, Dream, girl, I must say you look amazing, but that's no surprise."

"Thanks. And you look pretty good yourself," said Dream. There was never any doubt that the two of them were physically attracted to each other. They looked pretty good together, but for some reason Dream always played hard to get with Omar. She liked how things were, and she didn't want to mess up a good business relationship by throwing emotions in. Business and pleasure could cause major problems if things went wrong. She had seen it so many times with others, and she didn't want to take that risk. She could not help but notice how good Omar was looking in those sweatpants.

"I guess we can go to baggage claim and get your bags."

"No," said Omar. "I only brought one bag. I'm a man; I pack light. I'll leave all the heavy packing to you ladies. If I need something else, I will just go to the mall."

"Oh, OK. And see, I'm a little different. I pack light, too, so don't put me in the category with others."

"Well, you know what? That actually doesn't really surprise me because nothing about you is normal. You think and move differently; that's why you are my dream girl. I've been telling you that for years. There are so many things that make you different. I can't wait to see what has you bringing me all the way to the East Coast."

"Oh, well, you will see shortly, and I guarantee you will not regret taking this trip."

"Well, to be honest with you, just the fact that I get to see you is worth the trip. The rest is just a bonus. It's not every day that a man gets to see his dream girl."

CHAPTER 12

"Is this your first time in the Carolinas?" asked Dream.

"No. I used to spend my summers down here as a child. It's been years since I have been out here. My grandmother on my father's side lived further down south in a small town in South Carolina."

"What's the name of the town?"

"If I told you, you probably wouldn't believe me."

"Try me. You have never gave me a reason to question your word, so why would I start now?" asked Dream.

"The name of the town is Promised Land. The land was promised to our ancestors, and it was founded in 1869. My dad's mother wanted us to know our roots, so she would have me and all of my cousins spend our summers in the South. See, back in the slavery days, this was the land that was promised to the slaves. My grandmother and her family never moved away. I still have a lot of family that lives there now. To be honest about seventy percent of the population is made up of my family. Now the population is not very large; it consists of less than six hundred people. There is so much history in that town. Maybe one day I can take you to visit. You would love it, and my family would love you too. I think I will plan a trip down to see my family; sometimes we lose contact with those that matter the most. My grandmother always did her best to keep our family united. It's kind of sad that when you get old. You lose touch with relatives who you were once so close to."

"You're right about that," said Dream. "It shouldn't take a funeral, wedding, or family reunion to see your family, but sadly that is often the case. I know I am guilty of not staying in contact myself. That is something that I'm going to work on. When you go, let me know; I'd love to go with you."

"OK," agreed Omar.

As they rode back to Kim's house, Omar observed the scenery. The land was so different from California. The trees were beautiful, and there were so many of them. Out of nowhere it started to pour down rain. "I didn't realize rain was in the forecast today," said Dream.

"This is definitely a big difference," said Omar. "We barely get rain in Southern California."

Even though Dream hated to drive in the rain, and she could barely see, she was glad that Omar was able to experience the rain. He stared out of the window like a child would, amazed at the rain. He looked so relaxed as the rain hit the windows of her car. "I can't remember the last time I've rode in the car while it was raining." While he was calm, Dream, on the other hand, was so ready to get out of the car. She feared the other drivers on the road. It was raining cats and dogs; she could barely see, so she drove with caution.

"Thank God, we made it!" They had made it back to Kim's house. As soon as the door opened, they could smell the breakfast. Dream's stomach instantly started to growl after she smelled the food. Kim came to the door and greeted Omar as he walked in with Dream. She gave him a hug, and she introduced herself as Dream's sister from another mother.

"It is nice to meet you, Kim," said Omar. "You definitely have it smelling good in here."

"Well, thanks. I thought it would be nice to start our day off with a gourmet breakfast this morning." It was not often that Kim got in the kitchen, but when she did, she didn't play. Kim had prepared waffles, scrambled eggs, bacon, beef sausage, and bagels. She also had a variety of fresh fruit that consisted of blueberries, strawberries, bananas, and peaches. She wanted to make sure there was something for everyone. Not to mention that she loved fruit, and so did Dream.

Kim looked at Omar. He was quite a cutie. He gave her Larenz Tate vibes, but he looked even better. She was going to have to ask her sister why was she sleeping on Omar. It was obvious Dream trusted him because she had flown him all the way to the East Coast, not to mention that he was in Kim's house. She knew her sister and knew she was very selective after dating the wrong type a few times. Dream's cutoff game was strong; any red flags and, as she would say, "Application denied." Dream had been single for the last two years, and she wasn't really looking. Kim knew that in reality, Dream wanted to be married; she just wasn't rushing. She always said

God would send her perfect mate. Kim couldn't help but wonder if her sister was just plain blind because there was something about Omar's energy and spirit that was different. She had only been in his presence for a few minutes—but could he be the one God had for Dream? Kim decided to just observe and mind her business, but she was digging the way they complimented each other, and it was so natural, not even forced. She did blurt out, "So which one of y'all decided to wear matching outfits?" Omar and Dream looked at each other and smiled.

They both said, "This just happened; it wasn't planned."

"Wow, that's interesting," said Kim as she smiled.

"Omar, you can sit your bag down, and if you want, you're welcome to stay here. If not, I will get you a room at the Embassy."

"I'm fine here if that's OK with y'all. I don't want to invade your space."

"Don't be silly," said Dream. "We invited you here; I just want you to be comfortable."

Omar placed his bag on the floor in the living room. Everyone washed their hands, made plates, and then sat down to eat.

"That was delicious," said Omar. "Now that's southern hospitality."

"Yes, you're right about that. Thanks for breakfast, Kim. I'm full now. I'll clean the kitchen since you cooked." They were all about teamwork. Omar was observing this and liked the bond they had.

"OK, y'all. So let's see what we've got here." Kim went and got the jewelry and put everything on the table. The look on Omar's face was priceless.

Then he said, "Did y'all rob a jewelry store?" Neither of the ladies was too quick to answer. "Nah, but seriously," he said as he picked up one Rolex off the table. It was gold, covered with diamonds and surrounded by blue-and-red stones. "This watch alone is worth at least $500,000."

"Are you serious?" asked Dream/

"Do I look like I'm joking? I don't even know if I want to know how y'all got this, and I hope you haven't told anyone you have it. I take that back. I know you better than that, Dream. I'm going to say this, so listen closely: people will kill you behind this. I can definitely get rid of everything, but we've got to move it cautiously. These are high-end pieces. This one right here is a GMT Master II. I have a lot of connections in the jewelry industry. I also know that wherever these came from, someone is definitely looking for them. Y'all are going to have to put these in a safe deposit box today. We have no time to waste. This is too much money on this table; this is millions of dollars laying in our face.

"Just so you know how serious this is, we will go to the bank when they open, and I'm going to do a money transfer for $350,000 to your bank account. That is just for this one watch. I'm also going to make a phone call to my guy in Bangkok. He will get everything, and that's our best option. We have to move safe. If we sell this in the States, there is no doubt in my mind that it would backfire. The jewelry game can be more deadly than the drug game. I'm so glad you called me because I know exactly what to do."

Kim and Dream felt a moment of relief. This was the best news they had received in the last twenty-four hours besides God sparing their lives. Things just might be turning around. They would have Byron's attorney fees, investment money, and money to save. This was just from selling one watch. Dream kept calm, and even though she knew they had gotten the money from doing wrong, she was thankful for this money.

Omar looked at her and said, "You never fail to amaze me, dream girl. This one completely caught me off guard. When the bank opens, we will go and handle our business. We need to get that safe deposit box."

"I bank with Bank of America. There is one not far from here," said Dream. "They open up at nine o'clock, so we can leave here around eight forty, and we can beat the crowd."

"Do you smoke, Omar?" asked Kim.

"No," he said. "I don't mess around, but I do drink my Hennessey."

"Well, it's no pressure. I just wanted to ask since I'm about to roll up. That's what I do," said Kim as she walked outside on the screened-in porch to roll up. It was still raining, so she wanted to sit and watch the rain while she smoked.

Dream walked back there with Kim for a few minutes. "Girl, why are you playing?" asked Kim.

"What are you talking about, Kim?"

"You know what I'm talking about: Omar. He is fine; he has great energy. I can tell he cares about you. The man calls you his dream girl. That's so cute, Sis. I can see something with y'all, and not to mention, you two look great together."

"Sis, I really don't have a reason. I just don't want to ruin a great friendship; plus he lives all the way in California."

"Well, all I'm saying is don't block your blessings, Sis. He might be the one."

"I don't know, Kim. I'm sure he has a woman in California. Look at him. He is fine, and he is amazing."

"So? Look at you, Sis. You're beautiful, smart, loving; do not forget who you are. You are definitely a prize, and you're single."

"Yeah, now you do have a point there," said Dream. "Girl, let me go back in here; I just left him."

Omar had made himself comfortable. He was sitting on the couch, scrolling through the channels. Dream sat down for a few minutes, and they both watched the news. "Have I told you how good you are looking, dream girl? Have I ever told you why I call you dream girl? If I never explained why, it's because you are the woman that every man dreams about. Well, at least speaking for myself... you are the girl of my dreams. You are the full package; you are beautiful inside and out. When you get a man, he is going to be so lucky."

"Thanks, Omar. That is so sweet of you. I've been so focused on me and my daughters that I haven't really been dating. I've been slipping out here, playing in these streets. Now I'm ready for something different. I want to live for God. Whatever man God has for me will be a man who loves him. I'm not looking for anything, but when the time is right, I will know."

"That's how it's supposed to be. I'm so proud of you; I've watched you grow into a strong woman. Maybe while I'm in town, we can go on a friendly dinner date. Just give me a chance."

"I will do that, O. Plus you know I don't miss any meals."

Dream had just remembered that she needed to call Kay for Byron. She went outside and got his phone from the pocket on the back of her seat. His phone was almost dead, and it was an Android. She had caught it right in time because she did not have any type of Android charger. She quickly scrolled and got Kay's number out and dialed it from her phone. Kay didn't pick up the phone. Dream figured she may have been screening her calls, so she sent her a text saying she was calling for Byron. Kay called back within seconds. She already knew something was wrong.

Dream told her what was going on with Byron. Of course Kay was upset, but she wanted to know what she could do to help. She said she was going to put some money on her phone and put some money on his books. She told Dream she had been trying to help Byron start up his own dog-breeding business so he would leave the streets alone, but he was still playing around. Kay also made it clear that she was not going to turn her back on him, and they would get through this. She also felt the need to explain her actions a few days before when she was posted up at his sister's house. Dream told Kay that was none of her business, so she didn't have to explain anything to her.

"Thanks. That means a lot. After I thought about it, I was embarrassed. You know, I was thinking that was why I had not heard from him, that maybe he was upset. Well, thanks for letting me know, and please, when you talk to him, let him know I'll have money on my phone, and I love him."

"OK, I sure will. You take care of yourself; I'll talk to you later."

When Dream hung up, it was almost time for the bank to open up, so she went to see if Kim was ready.

CHAPTER 13

"Good morning," said the lady at the front door of the bank as Omar walked in. "How can we help you today?" she asked.

"I would like to speak to a financial adviser."

"I can help you with that, sir. Please sign in, and someone will be right with you."

Omar took a seat while he waited patiently. Dream had also walked inside, and she was asking about adding a safe deposit box to her account. She was also told to sign in and have a seat. A well-dressed middle-aged woman came and called Omar. He followed her to her office. She then asked, "What brings you in today?"

"I actually need to transfer some money over to another account. It is a large amount, so I wanted to make the process as simple as possible. I also need to know what my daily transfer limit is," stated Omar.

"I will be happy to take a look into your account and get that information for you. It says here that your limit is set for $500,000 daily."

"OK, great. Do you mind if I step out for a moment and get the account information for the one that I will be transferring the funds over to?"

"No, sir. Take your time; I will be right here." Omar could detect that she was flirting while still trying to remain professional; it was all in her eyes. Not for one minute did he entertain her low-key flirting; he kept it strictly business. He walked back into the waiting area, looking for Dream, but she was gone. A gentleman walked through as Omar was looking around and asked him if he could help him with something. "I'm already working with someone, but I was actually looking for a friend. We came together, but I don't see her, and I need to ask her a question."

The man smiled and asked, "Do you mind giving me your friend's name?"

At first Omar thought it sounded kind of strange that the banker wanted such personal information, so he hesitated. The banker quickly explained his reason for asking. He had a young lady in his office he was working with, and for some reason, he thought she may have been the person that Omar was looking for. Omar did think of the fact that he and Dream were wearing very similar outfits, so it wasn't hard to conclude that they were together. He spoke up and said, "Dream Zale."

The banker smiled and said, "Yes, that is her. She is in my office. Follow me." When they got to the office, Dream was sitting patiently. She looked surprised to see Omar walk back in.

Omar quickly asked her for the account information that he would be transferring the money to. "You can send it to my checking, and then I will move it accordingly." The banker printed out a paper with Dream's account information and passed it to Omar.

"Thank you," he said as he took the paper and left the office. Omar walked back into the office of the financial adviser.

"Thanks for your patience. I was able to get the information I needed."

"OK, wonderful. I will go ahead and process that for you now, Mr. Jackson. So how much would you like to transfer today?"

"I'm going to do the maximum amount of $500,000 today, and it will be going to this account." He passed her the paper with Dream's account information. The adviser had a look of shock on her face, but she followed Omar's instructions.

"I am completing the transfer now, but it may take up to seventy-two hours before the funds are completely available in the other account, so don't be alarmed. It will show as processing; this is a large amount, so it may take the full seventy-two hours."

"OK. That is fine. Can you please give me some sort of receipt to document this transaction?"

"Yes, certainly, Mr. Jackson. It is actually printing out right now."

"Thank you so much for your assistance this morning," said Omar.

"Of course, Mr. Jackson. It has been my pleasure, and if you need anything, don't hesitate to call me."

"OK, thank you. Have a nice day," said Omar as he made his exit from her office.

Dream and Omar were both finishing up at the same time. He could see she had the keys to the safe deposit box in her hands. This morning was moving smoothly and productively.

They both exited the bank, and Kim was sitting in the car. Dream's phone was beeping; it was a banking alert for her online banking. She looked at her phone and said, "Wait a minute; something is wrong here. This is saying I have a pending deposit for $500,000. You said $350,000."

"I know what I said. I wasn't sure of my transfer limit, but I found out, and so that's what I sent."

"Omar, are you sure? This is a lot of money."

"Yes, I'm sure. I will probably sell that watch for $800,000. That still gives me a $300,000 profit. I'm not going to shit you; I want all of us to win."

"Wow," said Dream. "God is showing out this morning. I'm almost speechless; give me a hug. Thank you so much, friend. Oh my God, thank you."

"You're welcome, dream girl. This is just the beginning. Some major things are going to transpire for all of us."

When they got back into the car, Dream immediately shared the news with Kim. Kim was now speechless, which was not often. Dream pulled the calculator up on her phone and did the math. "We all get $166,700, but that is actually $1,000 over. I didn't like the original number, $166,666, so y'all get a few dollars." Dream was big on numbers, and she wasn't about to play with the devil's numbers.

"As a matter of fact, let's do it like this. I'll take Byron's attorney fees off the top, and then we will split three ways from there. Max is charging $35,000, and I already gave him $7,000. That leaves us to owe $28,000. After we pay Max, we have $472,000 to split, which will give us $157,333 apiece. I like that number sequence much better. The numbers 333 represent growth in a positive direction. It's time for us to grow and glow, baby."

Dream looked at Kim and smiled. Kim looked at Omar and said, "Thank you. I guess you are our new business partner—because we've got more." She laughed.

"You're welcome, but I have to say thank y'all because we are all going to eat big; just watch."

"I don't have to watch." Kim laughed. "We are already eating."

CHAPTER 14

"Hey, Max. I'm sorry I missed your calls last night. I went to bed early."

"It's OK, Dream. There is no need for you to apologize. I can imagine that you were tired. I wanted to give you an update on Byron. First of all he has been transported to Raleigh since they have that hold on him. The charge is for a missed court date on a marijuana charge that is a misdemeanor, so it's not very serious; they just have to serve him with the warrant. He will most likely be back in a few days once he has been served and appears in front of a judge. After speaking with him yesterday, things may not be quite as bad as they seem. I'd rather go more into detail in person, but this is turning into a self-defense case at this point."

Dream could only imagine what kind of story Byron had come up with. She knew how he thought, and his freedom was on the line, so he was going to fight for it. The only witness they had was now dead, so she knew he was using that to his advantage. The man who had lost his life couldn't tell his version of the story. So Byron was going to create his own. Dream felt bad about what happened, but it could not be changed, and she didn't want to see Byron lose his life to this bad decision they all had made. "I can come by and meet with you sometime today if you have an opening."

"Of course I do. Can you be here this afternoon at four o'clock?"

"I sure can, and thanks again for everything," said Dream as she hung up the phone.

Omar had walked up while Dream was on the phone. Dream knew that he had most likely heard parts of her conversation. They had brought Byron's name up several times, so she was sure he was wondering who Byron was. Since Omar was now involved, she decided she had to let him in on the full story. "So I never told you exactly how we got the jewelry, but I'm going to give you the scoop, and that's the short version. So my friend Byron, who has been like a brother for years, was dealing with this chick. She decided to put him on to the guy she was dating. Yeah, I already know what you are thinking. I'll say it myself: that bitch ain't shit. You know I don't like calling a woman out her name, but she is no woman. Everything she did falls in the category of being a female dog. I never met her and have no desire to. She is a low-life, grimy muthafucka. I have no respect for someone like her.

"Anyways, let me get to the point. She gave Byron the heads-up that the man was leaving and told him all that he could get. I drove, and Byron and Kim went inside. The boyfriend somehow found out that the chick was planning to set him up, so he stayed in the house and waited. When Byron and Kim went inside, they split up, thinking no one was inside. Well, to Byron's surprise, the boyfriend came out shooting at him; they had a shoot-out. The boyfriend got shot, and the police surrounded Byron. Kim managed to get away, and when she got away, she also got away with a big bag of jewelry she had gotten from a chest in one of the bedrooms. Now Byron is in jail, charged with first-degree murder. That is why everything we make is being split three ways. I'm so glad I have the rest of the money for his attorney. I retained his attorney yesterday, who is one of the best in the city, if not the best. In my opinion he is the best."

"Damn, that's a lot, dream girl. I already knew it was something serious when you and Kim showed me the jewelry. Those are no ordinary pieces. Whoever the dead boyfriend was is well connected. What do you know about him?"

"I don't know much except I do know his name is Badrick, and he was Jamaican. He was living like a king in a house that looks like a mansion."

"OK, well, I'll see what I can find out about him, and I need you to do the same. I don't want you or Kim in any danger. I'm glad you let me know because I was not going to ask you."

"I know," said Dream, "but I've always been completely honest with you, and I don't plan to stop now. We may have lost contact for a while, but I've always been able to trust you, and I want you to be able to trust me."

"Dream, look at me." Omar looked her straight in the eyes. "I'm glad that you trust me, and I promise I'll never give you any reason not to, and from this day forward, we will have no more communication gaps. You may not believe this, but dream girl, you are so special to me; you have had a special place in my heart from day one." Before Dream knew it, Omar had pulled her closely and kissed her passionately. She liked it, too, but she was so confused. What is happening? At this moment she didn't resist, and she kissed him back. She didn't want to ruin their friendship, but something about this felt so right. She pulled back and then looked into his eyes. She grabbed him and gave him a quiet, long hug. Neither of them said a word; they just stood there and held each other.

"I knew it," said Kim. "Even a blind man could see the chemistry between you two. I'm just glad y'all finally stopped running from those feelings. I've been standing here for a few minutes. I heard everything. I think you two are so good for each other. I love it. Omar, I don't even have to say, 'Don't hurt my sister' because I know in my heart you would never do that. You two are a match made in heaven; I see something special here." Kim said this and walked out of the room so they could have their privacy.

CHAPTER 15

"Hi, Dream. How are you today?" asked Lisa.

"I'm great, and I hope you are. I have a four o'clock appointment with Max."

"Yes. He told me this morning that you would be in today. I'll let him know that you are here."

"Thanks, Lisa." Dream took her seat in the waiting room. Max walked in quickly to get her. "Hey, Max," she said. "Well, we meet again. I'm glad you could get me in since I will be heading home in a day or so. Kim will come and meet with you when I'm not in town."

"That's perfectly fine with me," said Max.

"I know my girls are missing their mommy, and I am definitely missing them. I've been trying to get as much as possible taken care of while I'm here."

"Well, let's get to it. As you know I spoke with Byron. After speaking with him, I'm leaning toward a justified homicide or manslaughter. Byron was invited into the home by Kiana; she is definitely a messy girl. He also told me you have his phone. I will need those messages she sent him with the plane ticket and all the other messages showing they were romantically involved. This is going to make Byron's story look more believable. It will appear as if he was just going for a pleasurable time while the boyfriend was out of town. Somehow the boyfriend returned and started shooting, and Byron protected himself. It's simple, and that turns the tables of this case completely.

"I'm not quite sure what Kiana's intentions were, but if you ask my opinion, she is bad news. Byron said he was watching TV, and Badrick walked in and started firing at him. Luckily Bryon had his gun, or we would have had a different ending. He said Kiana had just left to go to the grocery store and promised him he was OK because Badrick was on a flight headed out of town. I'm assuming that when she left, Badrick saw this as his chance to attack. Well, the only thing was he wasn't expecting Byron to have a gun, and this turned into a terrible shoot-out resulting in Badrick losing his life. These are terrible circumstances. I place all the blame on Kiana. I'm going to be working overtime to get these charges lowered. I feel for certain I will be able to, but let me do some research before I speak too much."

"I can't say thank you enough, Max. I've just been praying for God to give him another chance."

"I know you have. Byron is so thankful for you; he speaks so highly of you. I know you have a heart of gold. I told him he's lucky to have you as a friend. So many people would have turned their back on him, but not you; you're different."

"Thanks, Max, and can you tell me, what is Badrick's last name?"

"His last name is Chambers."

"OK, thanks. I was just wondering. Do you have any information on Kiana?"

"No," replied Max, "but I will. She has not been seen since Wednesday. She seems to have disappeared. Her phone is going straight to voice mail, and no one from the club has seen her."

"I will see what I can find out too," said Dream. "Oh, I will also have another payment of $7,000 next week."

"Well, I see you are serious business. I appreciate your promptness on everything. It makes my job so much easier. I have so many clients that get amnesia when it's time to make a payment. I respect you not only as a client but also as a woman. You are a woman of integrity. In today's world, sad to say, that's rare. Oh, I almost forgot; Tamia asked me to give you these." Max passed Dream two tickets to a women's empowerment conference with Tamia Banks as the main speaker. The conference was being held in Las Vegas.

"Oh, wow. Tell her I said thank you. I will be there, and Kim will be with me. Please tell her I said thanks for thinking of me. I am so proud of her, and I always enjoy her conferences. She is full of wisdom. It will be an honor to be in attendance."

"I'm not sure if you realize it or not, but you are one of Tamia's favorite people. She always speaks so highly of you. I'm so proud of her. She took that leap of faith, and God has pushed her to the limit. I love to see my wife reaching the lives of millions in a positive way. It gives me so much joy to see her walking in her calling.

God could not have picked a better wife for me. God pours into her, and she pours into me. I could go on and on about her all day." Max's face was lit up as he spoke of his wife.

"Well, please don't forget to thank her, and give her a hug for me. Tell her I will see her in Vegas."

"I sure will, Dream, and you have a good day."

"Good is an understatement, Max. This day has been awesome already. God has been showing up and showing out since I opened my eyes this morning."

When Dream got back into the car, she called Ann. Dream didn't like to go too long without talking to her girls. She had spoken with Ann yesterday, but the girls were asleep. "Hey, Auntie, what are y'all doing?"

"We just came in; they wanted to ride those dirt bikes. They almost gave me a heart attack on those things. Especially Hope...she wants to take off. I told them they going to wait until you get home; they tore my nerves up. Faith rides slow, but she still scares me. Why did you buy those things, Dream?"

"I want them to know how to ride. You know I'm a bike kind of lady, and if they learn while they are young, they will be skilled."

"I understand, but you're going to have to be their instructor. I don't want them getting hurt on my watch. Hope hears me on the phone with you, and she is standing here, looking in my mouth."

"Put my baby on the phone." Dream and Hope stayed on the phone for a few minutes, then she passed it to Faith. Those girls loved their mother more than anything in this world, and she loved them the same. Dream had promised to do something special with them when she got back home. Both of the girls were excited just from the sound of Dream's voice. She didn't want to tell them the exact day she would be home because they would hold her to it, and she did not want to let them down.

Ann got back on the phone and told her that her mom had called. Dream usually spoke to her mom every day, but she hadn't spoken to her in a few days, so she knew her mom was probably concerned. Ann said she could tell Vanessa wanted to know where Dream was, but she didn't ask, and Ann didn't volunteer the information. Dream told Ann she would call her but might wait until she got back. "You know how Mama Vanessa is. She will be asking a lot of questions." Dream didn't want to lie to her mom.

"Well, I love y'all, and I will be home soon. It won't be past the weekend before I get back."

"OK, well, like I told you before, we are just fine. Do what you need to do, and we will see you when you get home."

CHAPTER 16

"Hey, Sis. Are you home?"

"Yes, I'm here."

"Are you still in town?"

"Yes, I'm here for a few more days. I've been trying to get as much done as possible while I was here."

"I'm a few minutes from your house. I was on my way to pull up on you. Really, Sis, I low-key had an attitude with you because I had not seen you."

"See, Sasha, you have got to stop that. I told you I was going to try my best to make it by to see you before I left."

"Well, yes. I'm here. We actually just pulled back up from the seafood market. Your brother-in-law is about to put some steaks and crab legs on the grill."

"Don't tell me that. You know I love when E. cooks on the grill."

"Well, Sis, he is about to throw down. You know you are more than welcome to stay."

Dream pulled up to Sasha and E.'s. They were already outside. She could see E. had been fishing and was cleaning the fish off. Sasha was outside watering her flowers and smoking a blunt. Those two had been married over twenty years, and through the ups and downs, they had pushed through. Dream got out of the car and hugged her godsister. They were always so happy to see each other. She was especially proud of the fact that since the last time they had seen each other, Sasha had completed nursing school. The last few years had not been the best for Sasha and E., but they had pushed through. Sasha was working as a nurse at the local hospital in the pediatric ward. E. had started up a trucking company, and now he had two trucks on the road. Things were looking so good for them, and Dream was happy to see them living well and loving each other.

"Girl, you better stay away from that fish table," said E. to Dream.

"Bro, that was my first time in that hellhole. That place is a death trap, and from what I heard, it's over for that location. I won't front now; I see why people go because I watched Kim make a quick come-up real fast. I was even thinking about trying to play it myself. If I ever go to another one, it will be in a different environment. From what I see, a fish table has no place in the center of the hood."

"Well, Sis, that's where most of them are. I've never seen one in the suburbs. That one just had a lot going on; you got out of there just in time. That's all I been hearing about, is how Ox and his boys started a shoot-out in there."

"Yeah, I heard something about that too. It sounds like you better stay away from them places too, Bro."

"I know it's not my business, but why are you still playing in these streets when your trucking business is booming? I thought that was your whole point, was to get out the game."

"See, Sis, that's why I love you. You always keep it real and straight to the point," said Sasha.

"Now I'm not over here saying I don't make mistakes 'cause I've been making some crazy decisions myself," said Dream. "But we all have got to do better."

"Maybe your brother-in-law will listen to you because I've been saying the same thing for months."

"Baby, don't start that," said E. "I always listen to you. You are my wife; if it was not for you, I know I wouldn't be where I am today."

"Well, you sure don't act like it sometimes. I just don't want anything happening to us because of you wanting to be greedy. God has brought us through so many storms, and it's not right to keep doing dumb shit. I could see if we were hurting for money, but we're superstraight. With that being said"—he took Sasha's blunt—"I'm done talking."

Dream and Sasha walked inside and sat in the kitchen, where they enjoyed a glass of wine together while they caught up on some sister talk. Dream had to tell her sister about Omar. Sasha had remembered Omar from years ago when Dream started taking trips to Cali. "I've never met this Omar, but you have always spoke highly of him. You know I just want you to be happy, and I know that you're going to make a great wife."

"See, Sis, you're moving too fast. I'm just saying we had a kiss, and it was special. I was riding listening to that old-school Total 'Kissing You' on my way over here, LOL. I don't know what he really has going on in his personal life, and I definitely don't want to ruin a great friendship."

"Well, OK, you will figure it out, but you do know a great friendship is the best foundation for a strong marriage. If it wasn't for me and E. being friends, we would have never made it."

"That is a good point," said Dream. "Well, we will see what happens. For now we're taking baby steps. Let me get ready to go so I can get back to Kim's. I had to stop by before I go back home. It's been so good to see you, even though we had a short visit."

The two hugged, and Sasha walked Dream to her car. G. had the grill going, and the food was smelling good. "OK, Bro. You take care," Dream said to G.

"You gone already?" E. asked.

"Yes, I have some other things I need to do."

* * *

"Hey, y'all," said Dream as she walked back into Kim's house.

"How did everything go with Max?" asked Kim.

"Oh, it went great. He gave me some promising news on Byron. He said he is now aiming for manslaughter or justified homicide. Byron has created his own version of what happened, and he also has some great evidence that may help Byron out tremendously. I have a really good feeling about this. Byron will be home sooner than we think; just wait and see. Oh, and I found out Badrick's last name. It's Chambers."

"What?" said Omar. "And didn't you say he was Jamaican?"

"Yes, I did," said Dream.

"Man, if that's who I think, it is his father has top rank in the Jamaican cartel. If that's him, they are members of the most violent drug gangs in the country. His father's name is Meno Chambers. Meno is serving a life sentence in prison. They are extremely dangerous and connected. That would explain the jewelry.

"It's hard to explain that Badrick was alone in that house. Byron was a rookie compared to Badrick and his family. Your friend Byron is lucky to be alive, and so are y'all. Didn't you say you were driving your car, Dream?"

"Yes, I was, but no one saw us."

"You can't be sure about that. They probably had cameras. You are going to have to get rid of that car, dream girl."

Dream loved that car and had put so much work into it. She knew if Omar told her this, she was going to have to get rid of it.

"Our main concern is safety, and we don't need anything tracing back. When you start problems with the cartel, that's a different kind of trouble."

Dream knew that they were in deeper than she had thought. "Don't start stressing," said Omar. "I will not let anything happen to either one of you, and you know that. It's good that we have this information, so now we know how to move. I don't want either of you to stress. I've got an army that stands behind me. All I have to do is give them the word, and they are ready for war."

Kim had her poker face again, and no one knew what she was thinking. She looked like she was just taking everything in.

"You know what, dream girl? If it's OK with you, I want to take you out tonight. This has been a crazy week; you need to unwind. You already know I've been wanting to spend some special time with you for a while. Will you please accept my offer? Please, pretty please. Are you going to make me beg?"

"No, silly," said Dream. "I think that will be nice."

"Great. Can you be ready by eight o'clock?"

"Yes, she can," yelled Kim before Dream had the chance to say one word.

"Kim, I don't know what I'm going to wear. I did not pack anything dressy, and if I go shopping, that could take hours."

"Don't worry," said Kim. "I have the perfect dress. I bought it because it was just so beautiful, but I can't fit in it. The crazy thing is I had already decided I was going to give it to you, but until now I had forgot. It's absolutely perfect, and I know you're going to love it."

"OK, well, I'll let you ladies figure that part out. I need to make some reservations and handle a few things on my end. Dream girl, I will see you at eight o'clock. This is going to be a night neither of us forget."

Deep down Dream was so excited. She was still concerned about the cartel, but she couldn't help but wonder if it was her time. *Is Omar the man God has for me?* she thought. She had been so picky for so long, turning guys down left and right, but Omar was different. The funny thing was, this wasn't going to be her and Omar's first date. Maybe the first time was just bad timing. They both had matured so much from when they first met years ago. They really knew each other now. They were friends, and most of all, she trusted him.

God, I'm going to let you lead this, and if he's the one, I know you will show me.

"This is it," said Kim as she walked in with an asymmetrical one-sleeved gold dress. It was absolutely stunning, and gold was one of Dream's favorite colors. She loved the way she looked in gold; plus it made her feel like royalty.

"Oh my God, Kim! I love it. That dress has been waiting on me, and it was meant to be here for me tonight. I usually don't believe in perfect, but everything feels so perfect right now. I hope it fits," said Dream as she slid into it. "And it does," she said. She stood in front of the mirror, looking like someone from a magazine. She played with her hair in the mirror. "I'm going to pin my hair up tonight."

"That will show off your pretty face," said Kim.

"I have a pair of see-through glass-slipper heels in my trunk that will go perfectly with this. I'm going to go ahead and take my shower so I can be ready for my date night."

It seemed like Dream had gotten dressed quickly. Maybe it was from the excitement of the night she and

Omar had ahead of them. Dream walked into Kim's bedroom, and Kim's mouth dropped. "Sis, you look amazing. Girl, you look like a queen! I am so excited and happy for you."

Omar had walked down the hallway and said, "Is that my dream girl?"

"Yes, it's her," said Kim.

When Dream stepped into the hallway, all Omar could say was, "Wow!" He was amazed. He probably said, "Wow," about five times.

Omar reached out to grab Dream's hand. Once their hands were joined, he started to pray. He asked that God guide them in everything that they did. He also prayed that God would allow him to show Dream what romantic love should feel like. The prayer was so intense, but most of all, it was genuine. Omar could feel something wet on his hand. Dream was crying. He wiped her tears and looked at her and said, "I never want to make you cry."

She couldn't stop crying, but these were tears of joy. She knew at that moment that Omar was God-sent. "These are probably the best tears I have ever cried," she told him. "You just reminded me of God's promise and God's love."

At that moment Dream let go of her fears and decided to enjoy the night with Omar. They headed out the door and looked at Kim, who was crying. This was such a magical moment; it had her emotional. This night was just like Dream had always imagined true love should be: magical.

To be continued...

Lightning Source UK Ltd.
Milton Keynes UK
UKHW020631071222
413498UK00006B/382